MAGIC
DARK AND STRANGE

ALSO BY
KELLY POWELL

◇—◇—◇

SONGS FROM THE DEEP

MAGIC
DARK AND STRANGE

KELLY POWELL

Margaret K. McElderry Books

New York   London   Toronto   Sydney   New Delhi

MARGARET K. McELDERRY BOOKS
An imprint of Simon & Schuster Children's Publishing Division
1230 Avenue of the Americas, New York, New York 10020

Text © 2020 by Kelly Powell
Cover illustration © 2020 by Miranda Meeks
Book design by Sonia Chaghatzbanian and Greg Stadnyk © 2020 by
Simon & Schuster, Inc.

For information about special discounts for bulk purchases, please contact Simon & Schuster Special Sales at 1-866-506-1949 or business@simonandschuster.com.
The Simon & Schuster Speakers Bureau can bring authors to your live event. For more information or to book an event, contact the Simon & Schuster Speakers Bureau at 1-866-248-3049 or visit our website at www.simonspeakers.com.
Also available in a Margaret K. McElderry Books hardcover edition
The text for this book was set in Adobe Caslon Pro.
Manufactured in the United States of America
First Margaret K. McElderry Books paperback edition October 2021
2 4 6 8 10 9 7 5 3 1
The Library of Congress has cataloged the hardcover edition as follows:
Names: Powell, Kelly, 1991– author.
Title: Magic dark and strange / Kelly Powell.
Description: First edition. | New York : Margaret K. McElderry Books, [2020] | Audience: Ages 12 up. | Audience: Grades 10–12. | Summary: Catherine Daly's ability to awaken the dead for a final goodbye goes awry when she and Guy Nolan, the watchmaker's son, seek a watch but find, instead, a boy whose return from the dead draws danger to the three.
Identifiers: LCCN 2020020464 (print) | ISBN 9781534466081 (hardcover) | ISBN 9781534466104 (eBook)
Subjects: CYAC: Dead—Fiction. | Magic—Fiction. | Clocks and watches—Fiction.
Classification: LCC PZ7.1.P692 Mag 2020 (print) | DDC [Fic]—dc23
LC record available at https://lccn.loc.gov/2020020464
ISBN 9781534466098 (pbk)

MAGIC
DARK AND STRANGE

CHAPTER ONE

WAKING THE DEAD WASN'T nearly so unpleasant as having to dig them up in the first place.

Catherine Daly paused her work to wipe the sweat from her brow. In the cool night air, her breath misted and the wind gusted at her back, tossing dead leaves up against the low cemetery wall. A fine enough night for digging, all in all. It had rained earlier in the day, softening the soil, and even without the lantern burning at the grave's edge, Catherine could see well by the quarter of moonlight. She was used to the dark.

Up on the cemetery's hillside, she had a decent view of the cityscape below. Invercarn glowed with soft light, buildings lit by streetlamps, their facades elegant and imposing. The knolls and tree-lined paths of Rose Hill Cemetery promised only the best for those moneyed enough to be interred here. Not that they could much enjoy it once the coffin was nailed.

Unless, like tonight, certain services were called upon.

Catherine looked around at the sudden silence to find her colleague had elected to break when she had. Bridget leaned against her spade, the point sunk into the dirt.

"Keep digging," Catherine told her.

They had an audience after all. Catherine wanted him going back to Mr. Ainsworth with nothing but the coin he still owed and praise for their diligence. Thus far, he had watched them wordlessly, keeping back a few paces from the grave.

Geoffrey Watt.

He stood with his hands clasped behind his back, chin lifted. It was an attempt to maintain poise, perhaps, but by now Catherine had come to know when a client was nervous. He wasn't much older than she and Bridget—in his early twenties, at a guess—and had approached Ainsworth just last week.

His little sister had died of fever while he was away on business. He only wanted to say goodbye. Whatever time he was allowed, whatever the cost, he would pay it.

Catherine pitched another pile of dirt out of the grave. The well-to-do liked to bury their dead deep. There were resurrectionists in the city intent on digging up bodies to sell to medical students. Mortsafes were common implements in Rose Hill—the iron devices were cast over a number of graves on the hillside, set to guard the dead until the flesh became too rotted to be of use.

The robbers found their prizes more often in the public cemetery on the other side of the river. Rose Hill was private, guarded; Catherine was aware Watt must have paid off the watchmen to keep their distance.

The night wore on as she and Bridget continued to dig. They passed six feet, then eight before Catherine's spade hit wood.

At the sound—a solid and unmistakable *thunk*—Bridget put aside her own spade and took up the crowbar. Catherine fetched her coat. Inside it was a piece of type. She rolled the metal between her fingers, looking down at the ground beneath her. Then—

"Only an hour?" he asked. It was a tone of voice Catherine had heard before. In it was a plea for more, but magic could offer only so much.

Watt was here to say farewell.

"Yes," said Catherine in answer. "Your sister cannot remain long in such a state of being. She has no place here, not anymore."

Watt inclined his head in a nod. He held his hat in his hands now, and his fair hair matched his wan complexion. Bridget loosened the last nail and moved aside the casket's lid. The girl inside was as fair as Watt, wearing a fine evening dress, surrounded by the pale lining of the casket. Catherine knelt at the foot of it, clutching her solitary piece of metal type.

It was a type piece that held an hour of her life. If she brought it to the lantern, she knew she'd find the stain across it. She'd pricked her palm earlier, marking the metal with blood. Now she set it on the casket's edge. Placing her hand atop it, she whispered, "Mary Watt."

Beyond the walls of dirt, the stars shone bright and dizzying. Catherine stood up, and the girl's eyes blinked open. For a moment, the two simply stared at each other. Mary was pale as a ghost, and much like one, she was still dead. An hour of Catherine's own ticking clock could give her only a semblance of life. It was quite clear—from her glazed eyes to her ashen cheeks—that she no longer belonged among the living. And when she spoke, her voice was thin and distant.

She asked, "Who are you?"

Catherine swallowed. Climbing out of the pit, she turned to Watt. "You have the hour, sir."

Watt made his way over to the grave where his sister lay. He was trembling. Once he was inside, the girl said, "Geoffrey."

Catherine met Bridget's gaze, and together they headed to the nearby cemetery wall, where they waited under the branches of an oak tree.

Catherine pulled on her coat and looked out at the city. By the time Watt had his hour and they filled in the grave, it would be near dawn. For now, shadows darkened the cobblestones, obscuring the places between the gas lamps and rolling carriages.

Bridget leaned against the stone ledge, arms crossed. In a quiet voice, she said, "Mr. Watt didn't need to hear you speak of his sister so unkindly."

Catherine gave her an assessing look. "I don't think telling him the truth is an unkindness. Mr. Ainsworth should be informing clients of such things."

"Perhaps," said Bridget, a touch uneasy. She didn't like speaking out against their employer, no matter how far they were from earshot. Her blond hair was coming loose from its pins, ruffled by the breeze. She had fair wrists, slender hands calloused from working jobs like this one, dirt under her fingernails. Catherine was equally pale-skinned and angular, her dark hair done up in a chignon.

Once Watt's hour came to an end, the two returned to the gravesite. Watt was embracing his sister, the girl limp in his arms. Catherine looked elsewhere as he lowered Mary back into the casket. When he climbed out of the grave, he clasped their hands in turn, seemingly unaware of the dirt staining his trouser knees. He pressed a silver coin into Catherine's palm, smiling despite the tears in his eyes. They were the same shade of blue as his sister's.

"For your troubles," he said. "Thank you."

Catherine cleared her throat. "Mr. Ainsworth will pay you a call tomorrow morning," she told him, "in regard to outstanding payment."

"Of course."

Watt lifted his hat to them, then left the cemetery without a backward glance.

When they were alone, they secured Mary's casket and took to heaping the dirt back in. Catherine touched the coin in her pocket. After this, they'd walk out of Rose Hill Cemetery, head over the bridge, and return to their room at the print shop. Gripping her spade, she sank the blade into the earth. She thought of Mary's pale eyes, her raspy voice. She thought of Geoffrey Watt clasping her hand, accentuating his thanks with silver. Soon he would blur alongside all the other clients in her mind.

Just another night's work.

CHAPTER TWO

WHEN CATHERINE HAD FIRST LOOKED upon the print shop, it was from her seat on her family's old cart. Her father sat beside her, holding on to the reins, his expression grim as he pulled the horses to a stop. It was early spring and late in the evening, cold enough to make Catherine's nose run. She wiped at it hastily with her sleeve. She didn't want Father to think she was crying. If she cried, he'd turn the cart straight around and head for home.

She would *not* cry.

"Well," said Father, sounding both entirely too lighthearted and quite near tears himself. "It seems a fine place."

"Yes." Catherine fought back the lump in her throat. "Very fine."

Indeed, it was. Four stories of neat, dark brick, lined with sash windows. There was a polished front door with a heavy bronze knocker—like something out of a story.

A fortnight ago, Father had written ahead and secured her a job here. Now, in the dim, watery streetlight, he told her, "You don't have to go."

She curled her hands together in her lap. Those were the words she'd said to her older brother the previous year, when he'd left to go work in the mines.

They'd had another year of poor harvest, and just two months back, a storm left their roof badly damaged.

Working at the city's newspaper, Catherine could make good money. Her family knew that as well as she did.

"I'll manage." Her voice came out high, trembling, and that wouldn't do. She said again, "I'll manage," and this time she spoke clear so as to make it true.

Father got down off the cart to tie up the horses. Catherine followed and reached up to stroke their necks.

"You must write," said Father. "And if you . . . if you wish to come home, for whatever reason, for *any* reason, Catherine—"

"I know." She suspected she wouldn't be seeing home again for some time. "I'll write."

He went around to retrieve her trunk from the back of the cart, and Catherine looked about the cobblestone street. Everything was rain-dark and slick; the smell of the river hung heavy in the air. It was so far from the green fields she knew, the clean, wet earth and the open sky. But it was home to her now.

She put her shoulders back, lifted her chin. Father appeared carrying her trunk, and she walked alongside him to knock on the door.

Two years had passed since then.

On the third floor of the print shop, Catherine sat at her desk in the room she shared with Bridget. Early-morning light shone over papers and inkpots through the leaded rectangles dividing the window glass. There wasn't time to go to bed after returning from the cemetery, and the piece of type she'd used to wake Mary Watt was still tucked in her coat. It was one of several Mr. Ainsworth had purchased from Stewart and Sons type foundry. A space, blank of any letter, crafted finely and made to be susceptible to magic.

She took up the letter she'd written to her family the night before and sealed it in an envelope, intent on bringing it to the post office later.

There were things she hadn't realized back when she'd started working here. The *Invercarn Chronicle* printed all sorts—local news and events, shipping news, a wide range of advertisements— but Catherine was often tasked with printing the obituaries. And for the first year, she hadn't worked any graveyard shifts. Since the recent establishment of the newspaper across town—the *Journal*—Mr. Ainsworth had introduced the farewell service as another means of profit. It wasn't something put into the advertisements, but word of mouth brought clients to the door.

Catherine stood up and attempted once more to scrub the grave dirt from her nails. Along with the desk and the washstand, there were two wrought-iron beds on either side of the room, two chests of drawers, two bedside tables spotted with dried candle wax. The wallpaper was peeling in parts where it met the ceiling, but altogether it was clean and dry, with a view of the street below. She pinned up her hair and smoothed her hands over her dress before making her way down to the print floor.

Light came in through the front windows, illuminating tall sheaves of paper and type cabinets, tins of ink and composing sticks. It lent a gilded quality to the room, as lovely as gold leaf, and gleamed across the iron hand presses. Printed sheets were hung to dry on racks along the ceiling. Work desks were piled with tidy stacks of paper, information to be typeset and printed. A few employees were already behind them, composing sticks in hand or scratching down notes with their dip pens.

Catherine took an ink-stained apron off a peg and slipped it on. She pulled free a type case from one of the cabinets, carrying it over to her desk. With the first of several death notices before her, she began composing type, adding letter after letter to the composing stick she held.

She said, "Good morning, Spencer," as her foreman walked by her desk.

He stopped. "Morning, Catherine. Last night went well, I take it?"

She nodded, holding back a yawn. Her shifts at the cemetery were infrequent enough she didn't much mind the sleeplessness that came part and parcel with the extra pay. Spencer folded his arms, his head tilted to the side. With his brown hair slicked back and the sleeves of his shirt rolled up, he looked neat and managerial despite his youth. He was twenty-two now, once a compositor himself, before Ainsworth promoted him. It was Spencer Carlyle who had answered the door when she had first arrived. She could still recall that younger version of him: the bright snap of ambition in his eyes.

He asked, "And are you well?"

Once, when Catherine was a child, she'd seen a man in town selling enchanted keys that could open any lock. She remembered how her grandmother had guided her away, telling her magic couldn't darn stockings or mend holes in the roof and it was best to attend to more practical things. Catherine's parents quite agreed. So did Catherine herself. Yet here she was, in the city, making use of it. At least it gave people a chance to say goodbye. Even so, her magic was faint and fleeting—she couldn't bring anyone back to life, after all. There were times she felt she ought to notice the absence of the hours she'd lost bringing back the dead, to be able to root around and find the hollows, like gaps from missing teeth.

She told Spencer, "Perfectly so," and cast her eyes back down to her work. He tapped his knuckles against the desk and left her to it.

The print floor was soon filled with mechanical clatter, the swish of paper, the squeak of ink rollers. Catherine conveyed the lines on her composing stick to a metal chase. There were blocks of wood, furniture pieces, made to hold the type in place. Once the news was typeset, she'd lock it up tight with a quoin key, before carrying the completed forme over to the press to be inked and printed.

From across the shop, the front door opened, the bell above it chiming as Jonathan Ainsworth stepped inside, a cold gust of city air following in his wake. Catherine set down her composing stick. His gray eyes alighted upon her as he removed his gloves. In his well-tailored day suit, he looked sharp as cut glass. "Follow me, please, Miss Daly."

Catherine folded her hands in front of her as she shadowed him up the stairs. The *Chronicle* was once a maze to her, the openness of the print floor at odds with the corridors and locked rooms of the upper floors. The staircase was steep and narrow, lit by gas lamps in brackets along the wall. The second floor was where they took meals, the third made up of rooms for lodging, while the fourth contained the newspaper's archives, as well as Ainsworth's office. It was a grand room positioned at the front of the building, with a fireplace and several armchairs, a large window overlooking the street. Through it, omnibuses and private carriages vied for space as they sped along, rattling to and fro on the narrow roads. They crossed the dark, winding stretch of the river by way of North Bridge, to where the copper-clad spires and peaked roofs of finer establishments prevailed.

Ainsworth slipped off his coat, placed it over the chair back, and took a seat behind his lacquered desk. He lived in that moneyed district across the river, and he'd likely one day have a fine monument built for himself in Rose Hill Cemetery. Only during working hours did he venture here, to the soot-black buildings and uneven cobbles of Old Town.

"Mr. Watt was pleased with your work last night," Ainsworth told her.

Catherine inclined her head. "I'm glad to hear it."

There were about a dozen employees at the print shop who could work the magic Ainsworth required for the farewell service. Without them, he wouldn't have business in the cemetery at all— unless, of course, he could manage the same sort of enchantment himself. Catherine had never asked him.

He ran a finger along the edge of his desk. It was covered with organized stacks of paper, journals, a bookkeeping ledger. He said, "I've another job for you, if you're interested in taking it."

Catherine raised her eyebrows. "What is it, sir?"

The clock on the fireplace mantel ticked steadily in the pause. Ainsworth opened his desk drawer, pulling out a sheet of paper. "Mr. Watt paid off his balance, but it wasn't coin he owed. He had information I've been after for quite some while." As Catherine watched, Ainsworth took up his pen and began to write. "There's an unmarked plot in the public cemetery—the grave of a coffin maker. A timepiece was buried with him. I'd like you to collect it."

Catherine swallowed. She knew what timepiece he was referring to. Most at the shop believed Ainsworth had been looking for it since starting up the farewell service. The device was rumored to bring the dead to life—not as ghostly likenesses of themselves, as her magic brought about, but truly living.

"You'll be paid for the retrieval, of course. And I want it done tonight." Setting his pen aside, he looked up.

Catherine already knew her answer.

"Certainly, sir," she said. "I'll see to it."

When he offered her the paper, she saw he'd written directions marking the grave's location. She folded it and tucked it into her apron pocket. "Will that be all?"

"Yes, Miss Daly, thank you."

She went back downstairs to resume her work, but at midday, she returned to her room on the third floor. She put Ainsworth's instructions away in her coat, located her bonnet and gloves, and fetched the letter she needed to post. The sky was clear blue beyond the window, like it was in her memories when she thought of her family home. It lightened her heart as she left the room and headed outside.

CHAPTER THREE

INSIDE THE POST OFFICE, Catherine waited in line with her letter clutched between her hands. When she got to the counter, she recognized the boy behind it. Smiling, she said, "Hello, Mr. Douglas. How are you this afternoon?"

"Very well, Miss Daly." He smiled back, taking her letter. "And yourself?"

"I'm well. Have you anything for me today?"

"Indeed, I do. It came in with yesterday's post."

As he disappeared into the back room, Catherine put her hands against the counter. She was here once or twice a week; she knew just about every crack and corner of the place. The front counter was worn at its edge like her desk at the print shop, the glass pigeonhole boxes along the wall numbered in gold paint.

Douglas came back to the counter with her post. Her name

was penned across it in her mother's tidy handwriting. Catherine smiled at the sight, pocketed it in her coat, and passed on the money to have her own letter sent off.

Stepping onto the sidewalk, she started for the corner. There was another stop she wished to make before heading back to the *Chronicle*. She came upon it a couple of blocks later, in the midst of a row of adjoining buildings. Shop windows advertised the merchandise to be found inside, names and trades painted crisply above doorways. NOLAN'S WATCH & CLOCK REPAIR was a little green-fronted building with a brick flat above it, the curtains pulled across the white windows.

The bell atop the door announced her arrival.

She'd been here before on errands for Ainsworth. Like the print shop, Nolan's offered more than the name implied. It was whispered that Henry Nolan, alongside watchmaking and repairing, was a horologist who sold segments of literal time. And Catherine could think of no better place to go to find out if this buried timepiece was indeed enchanted. Despite herself, she was curious. It wasn't the sort of magic anyone at the print shop could accomplish. There were some who thought the device's capabilities were nothing more than rumor.

The watchmaker's shop appeared empty, and she was met only by an assortment of clocks on the wall behind the counter, all polished to a shine. Pendulums hung from several, while others were spring-driven, with brass inlay, decorative flourishes, gold edging.

The back-room door hung partially ajar. Through it, Catherine saw not Henry, but his son. He sat behind a worktable, hunched over what she assumed was a disassembled watch. With the slow, deliberate carefulness of someone used to handling delicate things, Guy Nolan set down his tweezers and removed the magnifying loupe he wore. He took off his wire-rimmed spectacles too, rubbing a hand over his eyes before getting up.

He didn't notice her until he came around the table to meet her at the door. He was tall and leanly built, wearing an apron over his clothes, his shirtsleeves rolled to his elbows. His brown hair was tidy, and he had a pleasant face—a certain clarity to his dark eyes, his expression attentive and curious as he regarded her. "Miss Daly," he said. "Good afternoon. What can I do for you?"

Catherine hadn't the faintest idea how to begin. "I've something particular to ask." She clasped her hands together, biting her lip. "Mr. Ainsworth has tasked me with obtaining a timepiece. And I'd like to know if the rumors about it are true."

"How do you mean?" A small crease appeared between Guy's brows. Then he brightened. "What sort of timepiece? We've several fine new pocket watches."

"No. That is, the timepiece he wants isn't here." Catherine felt around in her coat pocket for the silver coin Watt had given her, drawing it out and setting it on the counter. "It's buried in a plot in the public cemetery. I'm to dig it up tonight, and I'll pay you to study the piece."

Now Guy looked thoroughly confused. He rocked back slightly as if pushed. "You . . . You wish me to help you dig up a grave?"

Before she could answer, footsteps sounded from above. Guy's eyes darted up to the ceiling. Wiping his hands on his apron, he said, "This way, please, Miss Daly."

She thought at first he intended to lead her upstairs. Instead, they passed the back staircase and went out the door that brought them into the lot backing onto the building the next street over. It was little more than a bit of pavement, weeds growing heartily through the cracks. A washing line was strung up; Catherine very much doubted Guy wished her to see the nightclothes and drawers hanging there, so she cast about until her gaze landed on a flowerpot.

"Those are lovely," she said, just to be kind. Most of the flowers inside were brown and wilted, their stems drooped over the edge of the pot.

Guy's mouth curved in a half smile. "They aren't doing so well, are they? Too gloomy and cold this time of year, I'm afraid." He knelt before it. "I was thinking of getting some window boxes for the flat, but then, you wouldn't really be able to see them from the street." He shook his head and straightened up. "Miss Daly, how do you expect me to help you?"

"Have you heard of a timepiece that can bring back the dead?"

Scratching an eyebrow, Guy said, "That's an old tale."

Catherine grinned. "Yes, well, my employer thinks not, and I understand you're skilled in enchanting timepieces here. Could you determine what sort of magic it holds?"

His eyes flitted over her face. She wondered if he was thinking of the silver she'd placed on the counter or the reputed magic of this timepiece. In the distance, the city clock tower chimed the hour. A softer echo of it sounded from the closed door behind them, the Nolans' clocks striking in harmony. Guy looked down, twisting the fabric of his apron between his hands. "Perhaps I can." He glanced back up and swallowed. "You wish me to meet you tonight?"

She nodded quickly. "Midnight," she told him. "Do you know the willow tree on the grounds? The plot is near there."

Guy cut his gaze away from her, studying the brick wall of the lot.

"Mr. Nolan?"

"Very well." He spoke in a quiet, hesitant tone, as though fearful of being overheard. "If such a thing exists, I'd like to see it."

At his words, Catherine felt no small measure of relief. She'd never wandered the city's graveyards alone in the dark—lately, the watchmen had taken to patrolling the public cemetery almost as frequently as they did the private one—and it was a comfort knowing she'd have Guy Nolan's company tonight.

When they went back into the shop, Catherine took a last glance at the clocks along the wall. She wondered if some magic lay between the dial and gears, if an hour or so of time was conserved inside like the magic she placed within pieces of type. At the door, she said, "I'll see you tonight, Mr. Nolan."

He nodded back at her. "Good day, Miss Daly."

She walked out into the chilly November afternoon. A few stray leaves swept past on a gust of wind, the wheels of a carriage squeaking along over the cobbles. She slipped a hand into the pocket that held her mother's letter, reassuring herself it was there, before heading back in the direction of the print shop.

CHAPTER FOUR

AT THE *CHRONICLE*, there was always type to be cleaned and sorted. Catherine sat at a table on the print floor, a type case in front of her, its wooden compartments lit by the steady light of her lamp. It was quite late; she was alone downstairs, but she could make out the muffled footfalls and voices of others in the upper rooms.

This was the hour of day she liked best. When everything was calm and still, when she could let her mind wander, to think over things at her leisure and without interruption. Sometimes, oftentimes, she thought of home. Sometimes the ache of missing it was sharp enough to steal her breath.

She took a moment to admire the result of her handiwork—the type clean and squared away—before returning the case to its cabinet. Taking up the lamp, she headed for the stairs to her room.

Bridget was there, seated on a chair in the corner, darning a hole in her stocking.

Catherine set the lamp down on her bedside table. In the window glass, she glimpsed her reflection as she pulled the curtain closed. "I'm running an errand for Mr. Ainsworth tonight," she said.

Bridget looked up. "Can't it hold until morning?"

Catherine shook her head. Kneeling at the side of her bed, she pulled out the box she kept beneath it. Its contents were reminders of home, letters she'd received over her time here. The most recent one from her mother was already tucked inside. She'd opened it as soon as she'd returned to the shop that afternoon. It read:

> **Dear Catherine,**
>
> **I hope this letter finds you well. John has left for the mines**
> **again since last you wrote, and as of late, we've had only**
> **gray skies and rain. Is it so in the city? How are you getting**
> **on at the shop? Your father and Anne went into town**
> **yesterday and everyone there asked after you.**

Catherine usually found herself considering the letters during the night—as though to ensure they hadn't vanished during the daylight hours, to make certain she still remembered the life she'd had outside the brick and mortar of Invercarn. She lifted another envelope from the box. Opening the worn flap, she regarded her brother's handwriting. Now they were both working in the dark: he in the coal mines, and she, here in the city, unearthing coffins and waking the dearly departed.

She remembered the quiet morning when John left.

She'd sat across from him at the kitchen table, attempting to eat breakfast despite the lump in her throat. Tears stung the backs of her eyes, but she offered to help him load the cart he'd be taking to the mines.

"Don't fret, Catherine," he'd said. "I'll be home in the winter months."

But it wasn't the thought of his absence that troubled her so. It was where he was going. She'd heard tales of the mines in town—how dark and damp they were, how dangerous. Quietly, she said, "You don't have to go."

"It's a fair wage," John replied, as if this decided things. Her brother was ever and always practical. It was one of the many traits they shared, and it was her practicality that stopped her arguing. She didn't want her goodbye to be a discouraging one.

Putting her arms around him, she said, "Take care, John."

In the print shop, Bridget leaned forward in her chair. "Be careful, won't you, Catherine?"

"Of course," she said. And with a sigh, she set down her brother's letter and pushed the box back under her bed.

It was just past the eleventh hour when Catherine reached the cemetery gates. A sliver of moonlight illuminated the marble mausoleums and slanted grave markers, rooted trees and familiar pathways. She fetched the spade she'd tucked away behind the fence, swung it up onto her shoulder, and headed down one of the winding dirt trails.

In many ways, the city's cemeteries were as much a home to her as her room at the print shop. Invercarn Public Cemetery had existed long before Rose Hill, its age reflected in its surroundings. Here were the oldest headstones: crosses interlaced with knot work; stone angels, their arms outstretched, carved faces upturned in perpetual grief. Ivy grew through the cracks, twining around the monuments, masking their crumbled foundations. The walls of a dilapidated church loomed in the distance, its stones stained by damp and blanketed with moss.

The coffin maker's plot was unmarked, but Ainsworth had noted it near the old willow tree on his map. Gripping her lantern, Catherine placed her spade outward from the trunk, using its length to measure out the distance to the grave. Reaching the point written in Ainsworth's directions, she tapped her spade twice against the earth. Guy Nolan had yet to arrive, and with a sinking sensation, she realized that without him, digging up and reburying the coffin would take twice as long. Her eyes itched with tiredness; she looked up into the night, exhaling a clouded breath.

Then she got to work.

She pitched spadeful after spadeful of dirt aside, sweat collecting in the space between her shoulder blades and the small of her back. She cleared another mound of dirt and caught sight of a shadow beyond the grave's edge.

Guy Nolan stood at the foot of it, pale-faced and specter-like. He carried a spade of his own and wore a thick dark coat and a black top hat. He raised his free hand to touch the brim of it as their eyes met.

"Hello, Miss Daly."

"Mr. Nolan," she said gladly. Taking out a handkerchief, she wiped the sweat from her face. "It's good to see you."

He removed his coat and hat and set them down next to her lantern. Catherine was pleased to see he was dressed for the work. He wore a plain shirt and waistcoat, brown wool trousers. Joining her in the dug-up grave, he said, "Well, here I am. Is this how you usually spend your nights?"

Catherine let out a breathless laugh and pocketed her handkerchief. "Certainly not."

Guy studied her, his eyes black as ink in the darkness. "I know of the farewell service offered by the *Chronicle*—the magic you use in the cemeteries."

"Do you, now?" She leaned against her spade, smiling a little. "Yes, I don't much care for it, but I suppose it's why Mr. Ainsworth's interested in this timepiece." She angled her spade toward him. "I've heard you sell pieces of actual time in your shop. That seems quite the venture."

Guy turned his face away. "My father used to. He doesn't anymore."

There was an odd quality to his voice—an unexpected hardness—that made Catherine feel she'd overstepped in some way. She went back to digging, relieved when Guy followed suit.

His blade hit wood some time later. They cleared the remaining dirt, their breaths fogging the air. Catherine tossed her spade onto the grass and fetched a small crowbar from her coat.

"Let me," said Guy, reaching for it. "You did most of the digging."

She passed him the crowbar. The coffin was caved in a little from rot and the weight of the soil, the nails rusted and sunk deep. Whoever this coffin maker was, he'd been buried some time ago.

Guy wrested free the last nail and leaned back on his heels. He was flushed but smiling, holding up the offending nail like a prize. Catherine grinned in return. She took up her lantern and rubbed a spot on the glass.

When she turned back, Guy's smile faltered. In the lamplight, he appeared somber and thoughtful as a mourner. Standing up, he said only, "Hand me the light."

She did so, and he pushed aside the coffin lid. The two of them peered inside.

For a long moment, there was only silence.

Guy was the first to speak. He cleared his throat and said, in a rather delicate manner, "Miss Daly, are you quite sure we have the right plot?"

She swallowed. "I am."

"Did you not say he had a timepiece?"

"I did."

"Right." His attention returned to the coffin. "Then, if I might ask, where is it?"

CHAPTER FIVE

INSIDE THE COFFIN, the body was mostly decomposed, dried out and skeletal beneath a frayed suit. Catherine bent down, feeling along the coffin's sides. Nothing. She searched through the suit pockets only to be met with the same result.

The timepiece was gone. If it'd even been there at all.

She sat back, turning to Guy. He knelt beside her, pale and shivering as wind whistled over the grounds. "What now, Miss Daly?"

She wished she knew. "It ought to be here. This is it, the unmarked plot."

"Perhaps your employer's information was faulty."

They looked back at the remains of the corpse. Skin and muscle tissue stretched taut over the bones, only hollow sockets in the places where his eyes once were. His hair was dark and matted.

He'd clearly been dead for years, long enough Catherine couldn't tell his age.

She wondered how he'd died.

"Perhaps," she said quietly, "I can wake him."

The type from Stewart and Sons was still in her coat pocket, though she wasn't altogether sure her magic would work. The longest dead she'd ever brought back were in the ground six months at the outside. They were intact, preserved—not rotted to the bones.

When Guy said nothing, she looked his way.

He bit his lip. "Is that wise?" he asked finally. "He's not . . . He's been dead a long while, Miss Daly."

"Indeed, I might not be able to wake him." Her gaze flickered back to the corpse. "But he could very well know where this timepiece is." Reaching into her coat, she took out the blank type. She set a corner of it hard against her palm until it broke skin.

Guy whispered, "Do you know who he was?"

"No." She swallowed. "Mr. Ainsworth only said he was a coffin maker."

Placing the bloodstained type piece on the coffin's edge, she closed her eyes in concentration. She realized she didn't have a name to call on—no title to tie the coffin maker to his body. No sooner did she have the thought than the wind picked up, quickening her heartbeat. There came a sound like the breaking of crystal, thin and barely audible. Catherine frowned, wondering if she'd imagined it, just as Guy inhaled sharply and scrambled back, fetching up against the dirt wall behind them.

"Well, Miss Daly," he said, wide-eyed. "I think he moved."

She looked back at the coffin. And almost imperceptibly, the corpse shifted.

Catherine's stomach gave a lurch. She stared, transfixed, as the coffin maker's body began to flesh itself out—by nerve by sinew by vein by artery by organ.

A little awed, Guy said, "Is this your doing?"

"No," she replied, voice hushed. "This isn't my magic."

This was something new.

Sitting alongside Guy, Catherine watched it happen.

The boy—it was a boy, she saw, no older than them—lay inside the coffin as if he merely slept. He had a sweep of dark hair, a thin face, lashes that fluttered against his cheeks. His chest rose and fell beneath the folds of his suit jacket. He was breathing. *Breathing*.

Catherine's heart thudded.

This boy wasn't back on a temporary thread of magic. He was alive and whole, like death had never touched him.

The timepiece. It must be.

But where was it?

She got to her feet, eyeing the boy who, minutes prior, had been little more than a skeleton. Guy rose to stand next to her.

"The timepiece," he said, echoing her thoughts. "Could it have done this?"

"That would be my guess." Her voice came out faint.

"But how is that possible? It's not even here."

The lantern rested near the coffin, illuminating the cracked wood. Catherine stepped closer, kneeling beside it. She reached out to touch the boy's cheek.

His eyes opened, and she snatched her hand back.

The boy jolted upright, breathing hard and fast. "What is this?" His voice was shrill. "Where am I?" He looked down at himself, at his threadbare suit. He choked on his next inhale, even as he staggered out and away from the coffin. Alive as he was, his face shone deathly pale in the moonlight. He pressed back against the dirt wall behind him. "Stay back," he told them. "You keep right back from me."

Catherine straightened, held up her hands, even as her heart pounded in her chest.

"My name is Catherine Daly," she said. "May I ask yours?"

The boy stared at her, wild-eyed. He was breathing in gasps, air sawing in and out of his lungs.

Catherine glanced back at Guy. The two of them looked a nightmarish pair in the darkness of the cemetery, sweaty and filthy as they were. She imagined they weren't a sight that would ease anyone's mind upon waking from the grave. Guy's expression almost mirrored the boy's, both of them looking dazed and vaguely ill.

Catherine turned back around as the boy let out a nervous laugh. "I'm dreaming, surely," he said. "This is just . . . I don't—"

"You're not dreaming," Guy told him. His voice came out surprisingly steady despite his countenance. "You were dead."

The boy snapped, "If I were dead, I think I'd know it."

"It's fair to say you didn't," Guy replied.

Hesitantly, Catherine said, "Can you tell us your name?"

The boy frowned, raking a hand through his hair. "I don't . . . I can't recall." He went still, his eyes widening. "I can't remember. Why can't I remember?"

"That's all right," Catherine told him. "It might take a while to come back."

She hadn't the faintest if this was true or not, but she was willing to say whatever was necessary to keep him from panicking any further.

"What can you remember?" Guy asked.

Regarding him, the boy said, "Am I still in Invercarn?"

"Yes," replied Catherine. "We're in Invercarn."

The boy swallowed hard. He studiously avoided looking at the empty coffin as he pressed one hand to the dirt wall nearest him. His cravat hung crooked, his hair fell into his eyes, but there was no indication he'd slip from life anytime soon.

In a quiet, uneven voice, he said, "I'd like to get out of here now."

CHAPTER SIX

CATHERINE SCRAMBLED out of the grave with her lantern in hand. Guy came up after her, and together they helped the nameless boy onto the grass. He stood on the threshold of the pit, looking down. He seemed very much a part of the graveyard, in his dusty, worn-out suit, his features obscured in the dark.

Shaking his head, he murmured, "This can't be real." Yet the tremor in his voice betrayed him.

Catherine knew it must be a difficult thing to come to terms with. She shifted her weight from foot to foot, unsure of how to proceed. All magic centered on the basis of give-and-take. It was the reason why her life was shortened to give even a semblance of life to another.

And that raised a question begging to be answered.

Just what had been given to grant this boy new life?

When a gust of wind swept past, the boy shuddered in his thin suit. Guy held out his coat, but the boy stared as though Guy were offering him a used handkerchief. Suspicion glittered in his dark eyes as he crossed his arms tightly over his chest. "Who are you, then?" he demanded. "What do you want from me?"

At this, Catherine noticed Guy trying to catch her eye. She ignored him. "We were looking for something," she said. "It was meant to be buried with you."

His brow furrowed. He contemplated the gravesite once more and drew his lower lip between his teeth. "If I died ...," he began. "If I was ... buried here ... where is my headstone?"

Catherine swallowed. Quietly, she said, "Your grave was unmarked."

"Why would I ...?" The boy's chest heaved as he gaped at her. "That can't be right. None of this is *right*."

"I'm sure things will make more sense once your memories return."

Her words only seemed to agitate him. "How so?" he asked. "What do you expect me to remember?"

"I'm sure it's nothing terribly grim," Guy noted. He pulled on his coat, fetching up his hat from the grave's edge. "You built coffins, I'm told. An apprentice, perhaps, at your age. If you had no family, you simply might not have been able to afford proper burial."

The boy's breath caught. He said, "Family."

Catherine heard the hope in those few syllables. She had to tamp it down before it solidified into something that could be crushed. "You've been in the ground a long time," she said. "If you did have a family, they may not—that is, they may no longer be living."

Fear dawned on his face, plain even in the low light. His Adam's apple bobbed in his throat. "How long a time?" he asked.

"It's hard to say exactly, but by the state we found you in . . ." Catherine paused. "I'd wager twenty years or so."

The boy took a step back, tripped, and sat down rather abruptly. He was shaking, his face white as paper. Guy crouched beside him. "You'll need a name," he said gently. "Until you recall your own." And when the boy said nothing in return, Guy added, "I'm partial to Owen. How about that?"

The boy hunched his shoulders, looking elsewhere. "It's a fine name, I suppose."

"It's settled, then." Guy held out his hand. "Guy Nolan is mine."

The boy—Owen—hesitated a brief moment, before clasping Guy's hand in his. As Guy helped him to his feet, Catherine said, "If you'll excuse us, Owen. Mr. Nolan and I need a moment alone."

Guy caught her gaze and nodded. "Of course, Miss Daly."

Catherine put down her lantern, not wanting to leave the boy in the pitch dark.

She and Guy set off into the night, picking their way around exposed tree roots and flat stone markers. They came to a stop far enough away to be out of earshot but close enough to keep an eye on the boy standing inside the glow of Catherine's light.

Tipping her chin up, she studied Guy's face. He placed his hat back on his head, shadowing his eyes. "My father won't notice if I bring him back to the shop," he said. "He'll be safe there."

"That's gracious of you, Mr. Nolan, but it still doesn't solve the matter at hand."

"You mean the timepiece."

"I do mean the timepiece."

She could think of no other reason why this coffin maker was alive once more. If the device was not buried with him, it must be somewhere in this cemetery for it to have worked its magic as it did. Even after hearing the rumors, she hadn't put much thought into its existence, its capabilities. Such a thing would be prized beyond measure; it was little wonder why Ainsworth wanted it.

"I don't see how we'll find it in the dark, Miss Daly."

Catherine nodded. Yet her heart knocked against her ribs at the notion of returning to the print shop empty-handed.

Guy put his hands in his coat pockets, lowering his voice as he continued. "Perhaps, given time, he might remember something of it. I know someone with connections at the university. They may have information there about this timepiece."

"Who? A student?"

"Ah, no, not a student." Guy cast his eyes down. "He—he digs up bodies for the medical department."

Catherine's insides twisted. "A resurrectionist, then."

Most people considered the practice horrific. At least Catherine and her sort left the bodies in their coffins. At least they provided a comfort to grieving families. Resurrectionists unearthed cadavers and sold them off to anatomists in need of bodies to dissect.

"He could help," Guy said.

Catherine looked back toward the pinpoint of her lantern light. What she saw there—or rather, what she *didn't*—froze the blood in her veins. She grabbed Guy by the sleeve.

"The boy," she said. "Where's the boy?"

Guy snapped his head around.

"Oh," he said.

In the space between piles of grave dirt and Catherine's lantern, where Owen had stood waiting, there was only empty air.

The boy was gone.

CHAPTER SEVEN

CATHERINE NEVER SHOULD'VE let him out of her sight.

She made a dash for the grave, snatched her lantern, and held it high over her head. It was as good as casting light down a well—the darkness around them was unyielding, near tangible, and Owen could be anywhere among the trees and stone monuments.

"He can't have gone far," said Guy, coming up next to her. He surveyed the empty grave before turning his attention toward the front gates. In the gloom, the sharp-tipped finials were set in relief by the lamps lining the street. Catherine clutched her lantern tighter. She started down the path, peering between the rows of headstones.

Guy Nolan followed after her. "Poor fellow. He's likely scared out of his wits."

"Yes, I imagine so."

She headed for the cemetery's entrance, drawing closer to the rattling of carriages, the muffled calls and laughter from the doorways of gin palaces.

Owen, as Guy surmised, hadn't gone far at all. As they neared the front gates, Catherine found him standing to one side of the fence. His hands were curled around it, his forehead pressed to the iron. Guy moved forward and placed a hand on the boy's shoulder. The touch seemed to undo him in some way—he let out a shuddered breath, as if he might burst into tears. His voice was little more than a whisper as he said, "What am I supposed to do?" He turned, facing the two of them, yet he seemed to be looking elsewhere, his eyes far away. "Where am I to go?"

"I have somewhere you can stay," Guy told him.

Catherine gestured back with her lantern. "We need to fill in the grave," she said quietly. "Before sunrise."

Owen's knuckles whitened where he still held the fence. "Do not ask that of me."

"Mr. Nolan and I are more than capable. And the sooner we do, the sooner we can get out of this cold." Catherine looked to Guy. "Shall we?"

Shoveling the dirt back in wasn't as arduous as the initial dig. As such, her attention wandered from the grave to the boy it once contained. Owen stood watching them, shivering, his arms curled about himself.

"Oh, gracious," said Guy. He put aside his spade to remove his coat and hat, pushing them onto Owen. "You'll catch your death the very night you woke from it."

This time Owen took the items offered. The coat was a looser fit on him—Guy was taller by a couple of inches, his shoulders broader—and Owen dug his hands into the pockets, tucked his chin into the coat's collar, making himself appear even smaller.

"I truly died, then," he said, voice wavering. "I really . . . I was really dead."

"But now you're alive," Catherine told him. "Isn't it a wonder?"

"Not a wonder." Owen sniffed. "Magic."

"Not magic of our doing. It's a powerful sort that brought you back as you are."

Guy heaved another pile of dirt into the slowly filling pit. He said, "Miss Daly, you did make an attempt."

All she'd done was set down her piece of type. Guy turned to her, his spade balanced in his hands. He went on. "Perhaps your magic worked as a spark."

She looked away. God only knew what Ainsworth might do if he found out. She certainly couldn't tell him. The timepiece wasn't where he thought, and its magic had brought the coffin maker back to life.

Over the stone monuments, the first flush of dawn lit the sky. Catherine hadn't slept at all this night, and little the night before; she felt the heavy pull of exhaustion at her eyelids, her head clouded, that dizzy, unsteady feeling. She looked to Guy in the blue-black of the coming morning. He wiped at his eyes, offering her a tired smile.

"Come along," he said once they'd finished. "We'll head back to mine."

They left their spades behind the cemetery fence. Making their way to the watchmaker's shop, they passed by dustmen and lamplighters with their ladders and poles, extinguishing the streetlights. Guy stopped outside the shop and pulled a key from his trouser pocket.

Owen gazed into the darkened window. "You're a watchmaker?"

"Yes." Guy's tone was crisp, the pride in it quite plain. "My family has worked here for three generations."

Owen looked silently at the shadowed clockwork beyond the glass.

"Do you recall it?" Guy asked, unlocking the door.

After a pause, Owen shook his head. "Perhaps not."

Catherine ducked inside behind them. The interior of the shop was dark, the still audible ticking of the clocks made eerie in the dimness. It seemed a different place at night, somewhere strange and unfamiliar.

"There's a spare room upstairs," Guy told Owen. "You may stay there for the night." He took his coat and hat from him, setting them on the rack near the door. "What's left of it, rather."

"Thank you," said Owen. He glanced over at Catherine.

Even in the shadows, she made out the curiosity in his eyes. She spoke before it resolved into a question. "My place is at the *Invercarn Chronicle*. It's a few blocks from here." She turned to Guy. "If I may, I'll call on you tomorrow."

"Of course, Miss Daly."

She wanted to say something else. Something like *Thank you* or *My apologies*. She'd paid him to inspect a timepiece they hadn't been able to find. Now they were in this quandary, with this boy who hadn't any memory of his previous life, let alone the timepiece. But she said only: "Good night, then."

With her lantern in hand, she stepped back out into the darkness of the street. Tired as she was, the light seemed to flare and oscillate, spots dancing in her vision. She reached the print shop, the door opening with a groan under her hand. The presses were still, dark shapes across the floor, the sheets on the drying racks ghostly silhouettes above her head. She started upstairs and eased open the door to her room. Bridget was asleep, curled up facing the wall. Catherine placed her feet just so to avoid the creaks in the floorboards, not wanting to wake her. She set her lantern on the desk and changed into her nightclothes.

She needed just a few hours' rest, just a moment to close her eyes.

And as she got into bed, she considered once more what had occurred in the cemetery. Until sleep pulled her down into the dark.

CHAPTER EIGHT

CATHERINE SORTED THROUGH the type case in front of her, picking out another letter to place in the line forming on her composing stick. Her hands barely shook as she did so—a minor feat. Any moment, Jonathan Ainsworth would stride into the shop and find her lacking what he'd sent her to collect. The thought of it was like a fist around her heart, squeezing tighter with every beat.

She fixed her eyes on the type in her composing stick. Her thumb held the line in place, the nicks in the metal facing up. The written obituary informed her that the woman—Elizabeth Cleary, aged twenty-six years—was taken by consumption in the late-night hours. Catherine transferred the type from her composing stick to the chase. There was so much death in this city, printed in every paper. Lives snuffed out like candles, bodies put in the ground, to remain there so long as no robbers came to dig them back up—or, conversely, no magic restored them to life.

The public cemetery was now short of another corpse.

At the soft chime of the bell above of the shop door, Catherine stiffened. Ainsworth was early this morning—she ought to have anticipated that. She set down her composing stick, stomach churning.

His brow creased as she met his gaze. He said, "My office, please, Miss Daly," and Catherine did her best to clamp down on her nerves as she followed him up the stairs.

She walked into the office behind him, closed the door, and watched as he settled into his chair. He looked at her, and she decided to have out with it. "The timepiece wasn't there, sir," she said. "I dug up the grave, but there was no timepiece to be had. The coffin was empty."

Ainsworth's silver-gray eyes narrowed. He leaned back, considering her. "I thought my instructions were quite clear."

"Mr. Ainsworth, I had no trouble locating the coffin. It was simply—"

"Empty? What of the body?"

Catherine bit her lip. In her mind's eye, she saw Owen—how he'd stood in the cemetery, staring down at his grave, the fear etched across his countenance.

"There was no body, sir. As I said, there was naught to be found." And when he made no reply, she continued. "Perhaps the information you received—"

"Miss Daly," he cut in. "You would do well to give me the timepiece. If not, you may look for other employment."

It took a moment for the words to register. Catherine couldn't quite believe them. She stepped forward, knotting her hands together. "Sir, I don't have it. I did just as you asked, but . . . truly, I don't know where it might be."

Ainsworth was no longer looking at her. Raising a hand in dismissal, he said, "You have until day's end to turn it in. Otherwise . . ." He didn't finish the sentence, but Catherine could fill in the gaps.

She'd be out of a situation, out on the streets.

Though if Ainsworth really thought she had the timepiece, he might very well have her arrested. All it would take was a message to the police, and with his word against hers, Catherine hadn't a prayer.

"Sir," she said, and paused to rally herself. "Mr. Ainsworth, have I not done right by you these past two years? Send me elsewhere to search for this timepiece, but I cannot give you what I do not have."

His expression changed only slightly, only for a moment. He met her gaze, and Catherine saw Ainsworth as she knew him to be. Decisive, unyielding, hard of heart in an instant, like a cold snap blowing in.

"Be on your way, Miss Daly."

His tone was resolute, impervious to arguments. Catherine's pulse pounded in her ears, so that all other sound seemed washed away, replaced by the frantic beating. Throat dry, she nodded and retreated from the office.

In her room, she put on her coat, bonnet, and gloves, her movements numb, mechanical as the presses downstairs. She stared out the window—the glass fogged, early-morning condensation above the sill—to the blur of carriages and people below, passing by the *Chronicle* with nary a care of what went on behind its doors.

She stepped into the hall, headed down the stairs, straight across the print floor and out onto the sidewalk. She continued in a daze, tripping once, twice, on the cobblestones. The brisk morning air stung her eyes to tears; she wiped at them just as briskly as she came to the street on which the watchmaker's shop was located. The CLOSED sign was still upon the door, but Catherine knocked, hoping someone would hear and answer.

And someone did.

"Good morning, Mr. Nolan."

Guy did not look as though he'd gotten much rest in her absence. He was tidily dressed in a collared shirt and dark trousers, his waistcoat complemented by a golden watch chain, but his face was pallid, his eyes bleary with sleeplessness. "Miss Daly," he said. "I didn't realize you'd be coming to call so early."

She stepped over the threshold, lowering her voice to a whisper. "How is he?"

"Better now than he was during the night." Guy regarded her steadily. "He cried himself to sleep."

When Catherine said nothing to that, he turned away, leading her up the back staircase. The way was dark, close, the steps creaking beneath them. It reminded her of the print shop, and the thought was enough to knot her insides. She had until day's end to find the timepiece, but how was she to uncover it without an inkling of its whereabouts?

The stairs brought them into a narrow hall decked in flocked wallpaper. Catherine followed Guy through an open door into a kitchen. It was quite a large room, with a table and six chairs, a fireplace, shelves of crockery above the counter. Brass pots and pans were lined on hooks on the wall, and there was a kettle of water coming to a boil on the stove. The window was cracked open, the yellowed edge of the lace curtains fluttering over the sill. Despite the well-worn state of the furnishings, everything appeared orderly, scrubbed spotless, cared for in the manner Catherine cared for her own precious few belongings.

Owen sat at the table, but he stood politely when they entered the room. On the table before him was a rack of toast, blackened at the edges, the faint smell of burning hanging in the air. The morning's newspaper and Guy's spectacles lay in the space opposite, and in the light of day, surrounded by such ordinary things, Owen himself appeared less ethereal than he had the night before. Casting his eyes down, he said quietly, "Good morning, Miss Daly."

"Morning." She moved forward to take a seat. "How are you?"

Sitting back down, he said, "Well, thank you," though he bore the same marks of sleeplessness Guy did. He looked to be wearing some of Guy's clothes as well, slightly too loose on his more slender frame. His hair was brushed neatly, his eyes not as dark as they seemed to her in the night, but a muddy hazel color. "I must apologize for my behavior last night. I am grateful to you, and to Mr. Nolan, for taking me in so charitably. But I don't wish to impose myself on your goodwill. I will find work and a place of lodging and shan't disturb you any further."

She and Guy ought to be the ones apologizing. Owen would undoubtedly still be in the ground if it weren't for them. Now here he was, without his memories, trying to make the best of things. Catherine admired it, but that didn't stop selfishness from holding sway over her thoughts.

This boy was her only lead in discovering the timepiece and securing her job.

He couldn't just up and leave.

"Your consideration does you credit," she told him, "but finding work in this city isn't as easy as all that."

"Owen," said Guy, returning to his chair with teapot in hand, "perhaps you'd like to tell Miss Daly what you told me."

Owen sat a little straighter. "What I'd like is a last name. Calling me by the first is hardly proper when we aren't familiar with each other."

Guy took up his reading glasses, setting his eyes on the news-paper. "I've seen your skull," he muttered. "I think that makes us quite familiar."

This seemed to put Owen rather out of countenance. Hoping to console him, Catherine reached for the teapot and poured tea into his cup. "You may give yourself a last name, of course."

"Well, I . . . Yes, all right, then. You may call me Smith."

"Smith?" Guy considered him over the rims of his glasses. "Very well. Now do you wish to inform Miss Daly of what happened?"

Catherine folded her hands in her lap, trying to swallow down her own worries, which were aching to be said. Owen fidgeted with his teacup. "A nightmare," he murmured. "I thought perhaps—perhaps it could be—"

"A memory?" The possibility jolted her. "What was it?"

His mouth twisted. "Do keep in mind it was a dream, and a horrible one at that."

Next to her, Guy put aside his paper. His gaze was dark behind his spectacles as he fixed his attention on Owen. Catherine wondered what it was like for him—to have brought this boy into his home, to hear him crying in the night. Just as the watery daylight cleared away the strangeness of Owen Smith, so too did it grant Guy Nolan the appearance of composure, unruffled by this sud-den sweep of changes.

Shoulders hunched, Owen picked at a slice of toast as he spoke. "I was out walking—I don't know where. Someone—someone grabbed me from behind, pulled me into an alley. I felt something sharp at my neck." He brought his fingers to rest at the hollow of his throat, as if in search of a scar, but his pale skin was smooth and unmarked. "Then I woke up."

"And you didn't get a look at the person?" Catherine asked.

Owen shook his head. "How can I be sure this even happened?"

He stared down at the broken bits of toast on his plate, his voice turning small and choked. "Why would someone murder me?"

With a sigh, Guy took off his glasses. "Look here," he said. "We needn't get all worked up just yet. We haven't got any credible proof you were *murdered*, dear God."

His words may have chased away the night's phantoms—if the scene Owen described hadn't seemed so real. Catherine poured herself a cup of tea, adding milk, the tiny teaspoon clinking against the sides. "There is a way we might find out," she said.

Owen met her eyes, his expression despondent. "How's that, Miss Daly?"

She offered him a small smile. "A record of your death."

CHAPTER NINE

CATHERINE BROUGHT GUY and Owen back to the *Invercarn Chronicle*.

They stood across the street from the building, and this close to the river, the air was filled with the smell of dirt and rust and damp. Catherine eyed the window to Ainsworth's office. He seldom ventured outside of it during the workday, and he rarely visited the archive, which was where the old obituaries were kept.

Beside her, Guy took off his hat. "I'm not certain about this."

Catherine couldn't tell whether he was talking to her or to Owen. Perhaps both of them, though Owen didn't appear too keen on this endeavor. He'd had to borrow more of Guy's clothes, namely a dark coat and hat, which Guy had unearthed from a linen chest, taking a needle and thread to the torn seams before they set off.

Approaching the front door, Catherine asked, "Why do you say so, Mr. Nolan?"

"Well, we've no name, no date of birth, nor date of death. And I've got to head back to the shop around noon—I've clients coming by to pick up repairs." He checked his pocket watch, marking the time.

"Can't your father handle that?" Odd that she hadn't seen him at breakfast.

"He left earlier this morning," replied Guy. "He's repairing someone's long-case clock across the city."

"Well, I know my way around the archives. It shan't take long," Catherine said. "It's worth a look, at the very least."

Inside, she nodded to the employees who greeted her. She didn't stop to make conversation, leading the boys up the staircase to the fourth floor. It was still, near silent, away from the clatter of print work. The archive was around the back of the building, a long stretch of space crowded with tables and cabinets, old prints and files stowed away for safekeeping. It was the newspaper's own morgue.

The windows here were lined with soot and grime, the gray morning offering little illumination. Catherine set about lighting the lamps, the familiar task easing the knot of worry inside her.

"Is it all right that we're in here?" asked Owen.

She turned around. He stood next to one of the tables by the door, as if too nervous to step any farther into the room. Guy, meanwhile, was already scrutinizing the cabinets, the labeled drawers with their brass knobs, scratches in the wood finish. He tried one of the drawers; the wood was swollen, stuck fast, and Guy winced at the scraping sound it made as he tugged it out. Looking back at Owen, Catherine said, "Of course. The *Chronicle* has kept archives since it was established, a decade or so before your passing. We get plenty of visitors wishing to look through the old records."

Guy pushed up his glasses and flipped through the contents of the drawer. "Shall we each take a year? We can start with the papers printed twenty years ago and work forward from there."

"That's reasonable." Catherine glanced over at Owen. "Mr. Smith?"

He pulled away from the table and made his way across the room. His face was ashen, his eyes shining bright as coins. A thought occurred to Catherine, and she told him, "You needn't look yourself, if it pains you."

"No," he murmured. "It would take you and Mr. Nolan that much longer to go through it all. You've already done so much on my behalf—I truly am grateful."

Catherine bit her lip. She was at once overwhelmed with pity, caught in the fear that there was nothing to find, whether it be Owen's obituary or the timepiece. She set her fingertips to a cabinet drawer. She pulled it open, dust floating free.

They piled papers on a table and worked through them in a meticulous manner. By week, by month, by year. The obituaries were organized in narrow columns, and Catherine skimmed over the lines, wondering who'd set the type, who'd made the impressions. It was important work, the neatly printed pages telling of so many lives.

From the hallway came the sound of familiar footsteps. Catherine glanced up just as Spencer Carlyle opened the door, looking in at the three of them. "Catherine," he said. "I thought I saw you come up here."

She rose from her chair and headed over to him. He closed the door a little as he stepped inside. A nearby lamp on the wall cast light over his face, his blue eyes bright in the glow. "Why aren't you downstairs?" he asked. And then: "Is something wrong?"

She swallowed hard. "Mr. Ainsworth thinks I've stolen from him, is all."

Spencer frowned. "And why is that?"

Catherine set a hand on the door, shutting it the rest of the way. She spoke in a whisper. "You know the timepiece he's been looking for? He was given information it was in the public cemetery. He sent me to retrieve it, but—it wasn't *there*, Spencer." She could hear her voice rising and took a slow, steadying breath. "He doesn't believe me, so I have until the end of the day to hand it over, or he'll turn me out of doors." She stared at the light within the lamp. "It's not nearly enough time to look. Even if I find it, perhaps he'll want to get rid of me anyway, if he thinks I'm keeping it from him now."

Spencer leaned back against the wall. "Do you wish me to speak with him?"

Her eyes flashed to his. Hope flared in her heart like a struck match. "Oh, Spencer, would you? I'd be much obliged."

"I can't say he'll listen to me." He peered around her, as if only now noticing Guy and Owen. "Who are they?"

"Friends of mine." She looked over at their table. The boys sat across from each other, heads ducked, papers in front of them. "They wanted a look into the archives. We'll put everything back in its place."

Spencer said, "That's Guy Nolan, isn't it? I recognize him."

"Yes. I asked him if he'd study the timepiece. I wanted . . . I wanted to know if the rumors about its magic were true." Her gaze went to Owen, her insides twisting. She'd learned all too well of the timepiece's enchantment, the rumors proven real.

Spencer let out a sigh. "I'll talk to him, Catherine."

"Thank you."

He left, closing the door, and she started back across the room. Dust particles drifted in the air, caught in the lamplight, the spread of papers on the table marked with hard creases, ripped at the edges, pages worn so thin in parts they were made translucent. She took a seat beside Owen, and Guy looked up, questioning.

"That was Spencer Carlyle," she told him. "He's the foreman."

"Ah."

She reached for another paper, flipping to the obituaries. They passed some while in silence, before Guy asked, "Mr. Smith, how old do you suppose you are?"

Owen rubbed the back of his neck. In a tentative, hopeful tone, he said, "Eighteen?"

Catherine smiled down at her paper. She was seventeen, and he didn't look any older than she was.

Guy didn't mock his answer, but replied in all seriousness, "I just turned eighteen myself. I think you're perhaps a little younger. Fifteen? Sixteen?"

"Perhaps," said Owen quietly.

Catherine said, "Strictly speaking, Mr. Smith, you're older than either of us."

Guy nodded. "You've a point there, Miss Daly." He looked down at the newspaper before him, tapping his fingers idly against the page. "There was a boy of fifteen years apprenticed to a wheelwright. He died after a short but severe illness—it says naught else."

"They're all rather short, aren't they?" Owen replied. "It's difficult to know for certain with only a line or two." Lowering his gaze, he smoothed over the creases in the paper. "It would be a fine thing, I think, if someone who knew me wrote something kind after my passing."

Catherine carefully folded the newspaper she held. They could spend the rest of the day here and find nothing. Owen was right: The death notices were often short, with too little information to substantiate the murder of a coffin maker. She was still no closer to discovering the timepiece—and her time was winding down.

"Perhaps we ought to depart," she said.

Owen gathered together some of the papers. As he headed for the cabinets, Catherine made to follow, but stilled when Guy murmured, "A word, please, Miss Daly."

She looked back at him. "What is it?"

His brown eyes were the color of dark tea behind his spectacles. His hair fell across his forehead, and he pushed it aside, his mouth a thin line of concern. "Is everything all right?" he asked. "This morning—and just now—" He leaned toward her, his voice dipping low. "Is something the matter?"

She cast her eyes down, studying the grain of the table, the knots in the wood. "Mr. Ainsworth thinks I've taken the timepiece."

"What?"

"And he'll turn me out if I don't return with it by tonight. Mr. Carlyle said he'd try to reason with him, but . . ." She trailed off, running her fingertips along the table's edge.

Guy blinked at her. "Well, now," he said after a moment, "he hasn't seen it before, has he?"

Catherine knew just what he meant and she didn't like it. "Don't be absurd."

"It's only a suggestion. We've plenty of old watches lying around the shop. If I gave you one, and you gave it to him, will he know it isn't the one he's after? I think there's a chance he won't." His gaze drifted past her, and he stood up, placing a hand flat over his waistcoat. "Mr. Smith, there you are. Grand."

Owen pulled on his coat. "Will we be heading back to your flat now?" He clutched Guy's cast-off hat in his gloved hands, looking between the two of them.

"Yes, let's. You may even stay downstairs in the shop, if you like."

Catherine tugged on her own coat. She smoothed back loose strands of her hair and tied her bonnet in place. She turned down the lamps, leaving the room in shadow.

CHAPTER TEN

OUT ON THE STREET, the sun shone through a gap in the cloud cover. It was close to midday, and a crowded omnibus rolled past them, the coach painted green and yellow, the horses' hooves clicking against the cobbles. They started in the direction of the watchmaker's shop, heading away from the river, to the narrow stretches of smaller streets, the dark alleys that cut between them. When they passed the way to the public cemetery, Catherine couldn't help but glance back. It'd be wise to return before dark; if Owen was to stay with Guy, she ought to turn back and search the grounds alone.

Reaching the corner, Catherine spotted a young man sitting on the low front step of the Nolans' shop. His hat was placed beside him, his blond hair a stark contrast to the green front of the building.

"Mr. Nolan," she said, "who's that on your step?"

Guy paused on the pavement. "Sydney Mallory." Meeting her gaze, he added, "I believe I've mentioned him to you, Miss Daly."

And Catherine realized who this person must be.

Sydney Mallory was the resurrectionist.

In that same moment, Sydney noticed them. Getting up from the step, he set his hat on his head and made his way over to them. "Guy!" he said. "I tried knocking—isn't your father in? It hardly seems advantageous to close up every time you step out." Though he looked to be the same age as Guy, he was a little taller, wearing a dark-gray overcoat. His blue eyes alit on Catherine, and he doffed his hat. "Good day, miss."

Guy said, "Sydney, please meet Miss Daly. She's a compositor at the *Chronicle*. Miss Daly, this is Sydney Mallory."

"A pleasure to meet you, Mr. Mallory," said Catherine, though she wasn't yet sure of that. She wondered if he had a daytime profession, or if resurrecting bodies was his only work. Though she supposed if he did have another occupation, Guy would've remarked on it.

Sydney replied, "The pleasure is mine, Miss Daly," before his attention shifted to the remaining member of their company.

Owen looked on with his hat in his hands, so near the sidewalk's edge he was at risk of being struck by a passing carriage. Guy introduced him, telling Sydney, "Mr. Smith is from the country and recently orphaned. He's looking for work."

Sydney put a hand to his heart. "I'm an orphan and I get by all right. You must come to call sometime—the lodging house on Navy Street."

"Oh." Owen's gaze darted to Guy and Catherine and back to Sydney. "Thank you, Mr. Mallory. That's very gracious."

Guy took his shop key from his pocket. He moved to open the door, and Sydney said, "Shall I come around another time? I don't wish to intrude if you have company."

At that, Guy glanced back. His eyes shifted from Sydney to Catherine. It was clear to her Sydney had some matter to discuss, and if Guy were to make inquiries about the timepiece, perhaps Owen ought not to be present.

She said, "Mr. Smith and I were just on our way." She looked over at Owen with a smile. "Walk with me, won't you? You still haven't seen much of the city."

"That's a fine idea," Guy jumped in. "There's naught for you to do in the shop anyway, Mr. Smith."

"All right." Biting his lip, Owen replaced his hat. "That is, if you're certain."

"Quite." Guy pushed open the door. "I'll see you this evening."

Sydney bade them farewell, and Catherine ushered Owen along, guiding him down an alley to emerge on a main road. The sky had clouded over, the leaden color promising rain. Catherine didn't suppose Owen would be keen on accompanying her to the cemetery. As they passed a grocer's, then a haberdasher's, he cast a curious look into the shop windows. He said, "Mr. Mallory is a friend of Mr. Nolan's, I take it?"

Catherine paused beside him, smoothing a gloved hand over her coat. She thought Guy likely had many friends. He seemed a good sort of friend to have—so earnest and reliable, so set in his place in the world.

She replied, "A friend, yes."

"Hmm. He seems a fine gent." Clasping his hands behind his back, Owen turned to her. "Do you think I could make hats?"

Her brow furrowed at the change of subject. "Pardon?"

He inclined his head toward the haberdasher's shop. "I need to find work, some sort of apprenticeship. You said I was once a coffin maker, but—that seems rather morbid, doesn't it?"

"Well, I print obituaries."

He swallowed hard. Continuing down the street, he said, "I think I could be a good baker, if I applied myself. Or perhaps I could learn to drive a coach."

"I suppose . . . Mr. Smith, are you all right?"

Owen had turned colorless, his breaths uneven. Patches of red bloomed along his cheekbones. He nodded, took off his hat, and said, "Yes, I—I think I just need to sit."

"Of course." Catherine directed him to the front steps of a bank. She sat beside him and rested a hand against the stone step. "It's perfectly understandable if you're feeling overwhelmed. You've been out of the ground for very little time. Indeed, not even a full day."

"It's not that," he said thickly. "Well, not just that. It's—" He ducked his head, his grip tight on Guy's old hat. "You both have lives and friends and things to do and I *know* I'm a bother. I don't mean to be, but I am, and I'm sorry." Tears slid down his cheeks, and he pushed them aside impatiently. "I don't even have my own clothes to wear."

Softly, Catherine asked, "Where are the ones you were buried in?"

"Still in Mr. Nolan's flat." He let out a laugh. "They were quite dirty, and he said I looked like an old codger in them besides, so he gave me some of his."

"Now, isn't that a kindness?" Catherine did her best to sound lighthearted. "He cares enough not to let you go out dressed unfashionably."

Owen laughed again, but his eyes were still full of tears. Catherine placed a hand over his. "You're not a bother, Mr. Smith. Your bones would still be lying in your coffin if Mr. Nolan and I hadn't come along last night. It'd be cruel of us not to look out for you."

Owen gazed back at her. Hesitantly, he asked, "What was it you were looking for? When you dug me up?"

"A timepiece." Catherine let out a breath. "It was believed to be buried with you. My employer tasked me with fetching it."

He tipped his head to the side. "Was it mine?"

"I don't know."

Looking away, he scrubbed the remaining tears from his eyes. "If it was not your magic that brought me back, it was someone else's doing. Perhaps if we find this timepiece, we'll find them, too." Rain began to fall, speckling the stone steps, and he tilted his face up to meet it, closing his eyes and exhaling slowly.

Catherine sat with him a moment longer. The timepiece's whereabouts could very well be one of his lost memories. Rain dampened their clothes, but neither of them remarked on it, nor moved to get up. People hurried along on the street, umbrellas unfurling.

Keeping his eyes closed, Owen asked, "Miss Daly, how many coffin makers are there in this city?"

"I'm not sure." She watched as a carriage passed them, its wheels turning up rainwater. "But I know of one."

"I'd like to go there. If you'll show me the way."

CHAPTER ELEVEN

THE COFFIN SHOP SAT on a corner lot on a small lane near the factory district. It was next door to a cabinetmaker's, the sandstone buildings blackened with coal soot. Their respective trades were painted in faded capital letters above the doors. The rain had ceased, though it was still overcast, and everything was made damp and dark and slick.

"Here it is," said Catherine. She looked over at Owen. "Would you like to go in?"

He nodded, distracted as he glanced around. The lane was empty of people aside from them. Rainwater collected on the shop steps, dimpled in the middle from age and wear. They came to the door, and Owen reached out to set his hand on the knob. He peered up at the painted lettering before releasing a defeated little sigh. "Nothing," he said. "I can't remember any of this."

"Don't lose heart, Mr. Smith. Give it time—it may all come rushing back."

Owen's past might be found beneath this roof, his memories. And with it, the possibility of finding the timepiece. When they stepped inside, the place was mercifully warm and dry. Gas lamps were lit along the walls, hissing softly, illuminating the dark wood floor, the details of the flocked wallpaper. No one stood at the shop counter, and Catherine turned back to find Owen still at the front of the room. Two velvet sofas were by the entrance, a watercolor landscape of Invercarn hanging above them. It was a lovely painting of dark-brown buildings, the slate-gray sky, morning-blue shadows.

"Say now, what are you doing in here?"

Catherine grimaced at that tone of voice. Looking over, she saw a man in his early thirties in the back-room doorway. He eyed them warily, his mouth pressed thin.

Even if they weren't wet from the rain—making it obvious they hadn't stepped light from a carriage—neither Catherine nor Owen were dressed especially fine. No matter what Catherine had said about fashionableness, the clothes Owen wore were still noticeably secondhand, fraying at the cuffs. Catherine wasn't much better off, in her old coat and bonnet, with only a few petticoats to give shape to the skirt of her dress. Clearly they were not here with money to spend on an ornate coffin.

"Good day, sir," Catherine said cheerfully. "We're looking for someone who might've worked in this establishment some years back. May we ask you a few questions?"

"No, no, no. You're not here to buy nothing—be off with you." The man came around the counter to stand before them, arms crossed. He was clean-shaven and his ginger hair was brushed back, his work apron marked with oil and wood stain.

Owen stepped forward. "How long have you worked in this shop, sir?"

"Since I was a boy," said the coffin maker, gesturing to the door. "If you're looking for someone, you'd have better luck going to the police, eh?"

"During your apprenticeship, did a boy with my likeness work here?"

"How am I to know? Plenty have worked here over the years. Some stay on; some go elsewhere—I've not got a record."

"Sir, please." Owen's voice cracked. Catherine could only imagine how much he must want this—to be remembered, to know he once existed in the world. "If you could just think on it."

The man walked over. "You do have a familiar look about you." His eyes narrowed. "Is this a relative of yours?"

Owen stood motionless, wide-eyed and pale. His voice was faint as he said, "What can you remember about him? Can you—do you remember his name?"

"No. He worked here years ago, mind." The man scratched the back of his head. "Kept to himself. Quiet-like, you know? Then he up and vanished—never saw him after that."

Owen shared a look with Catherine. He raised a shaky hand to his throat, as if to reassure himself of his pulse.

Vanished.

So it was true. Owen had worked in this shop, at least for a time, and something awful had happened to him. A shiver crept over her spine as she considered again the nightmare he'd spoken of that morning.

"I'm afraid that's all the help I can offer. You go on now, the pair of you."

The coffin maker headed for the counter. Catherine turned toward the door, hoping Owen would follow, but stopped as he called out, "Wait."

He stood looking at the coffin maker. There was a desperate, peculiar light to his eyes, and when the man met his gaze, Owen asked him, "What's your name?"

The man tilted his head. "Reed," he said after a pause. "James Reed."

"Mr. Reed." Owen took a breath and nodded. "Thank you. I'm Owen Smith."

The man put his hands in his trouser pockets. "Right. Good day, Mr. Smith."

They stepped back out onto the lane, and the wind pulled at the ribbons of Catherine's bonnet. The day was settling into late afternoon, the chill in the air becoming crisp and cold as the light dwindled. Owen put on his hat, shading his eyes. Catherine waited for him to speak.

He said, "That man knew me. James Reed. He knew me." His words ran together, tumbling out. "Whoever I was—he knew that person. And I knew him. I was—I was quiet and kept to myself. That seems all right, doesn't it? I mean . . ."

"It must be a shock," Catherine offered. She eyed the darkening sky, the shadowed peaks of the buildings up ahead. It was the watercolor painting washed in gray, a motley collection of soot-stained brick and stone. The thought of the timepiece was incessant as pins and needles, but if there was some clue of it in Owen's past, they hadn't found it in the obituary pages or the coffin shop. Catherine imagined being dismissed from the *Chronicle*, but it didn't bear thinking on.

The day was not yet done.

"A shock? Yes. I suppose it is, Miss Daly." Owen rubbed at

his eyes. "My head is aching something terrible."

"We'll return to Mr. Nolan's and get him to make us tea."

He nodded, sniffed, and ran a hand over his eyes a second time as they turned the corner. She knew he was crying again. She passed him a handkerchief, saying, "It's all right," when he choked out, "Sorry," and, "Thank you," in quick succession.

Dry leaves whirled up in the breeze, fluttering across their path. Catherine shivered, the cold biting at her cheeks, but she only ducked her head, continuing on.

She still had the cemetery to search.

CHAPTER TWELVE

When Catherine and Owen arrived at the watchmaker's, Guy Nolan closed shop and led them upstairs to his flat. Owen quickly retired to the spare room down the hall, claiming a headache; Catherine couldn't blame him for wanting to be alone. Guy made him up a plate of cheese and toast, a cup of lavender tea and honey to help him sleep. Catherine bade Owen good night and took a seat at the kitchen table.

The mantel clock above the fireplace ticked softly in the stillness. Beside it, a painted miniature sat in an oval frame. It was a picture of a dark-haired boy—no older than ten—standing solemn-faced in a jacket and short trousers. Guy came back into the kitchen, and Catherine smiled, gesturing to it. "Is that you?"

He glanced at the portrait but didn't answer the question. He went and stood at the window, resting his hands against the sill. "Mr. Smith seems quite overset."

She sighed. "Yes. We visited the coffin maker's on Burnside Lane. The man there—he knew him from before. He said he just vanished one day."

Guy turned to look at her. He was silhouetted against the window, his watch chain glinting at his waistcoat pocket. "You do think he was murdered, then?"

Catherine swallowed. "Is that so hard to believe?"

"No." Guy took a moment to close his eyes. "No. Sadly, I find it all too easy to believe. And buried in an unmarked grave like he was." He shook his head. "I'll wager he had no one in the world to care for him."

Catherine pushed up from the table. She took hold of her coat and bonnet and slipped on her gloves. Her heart remained steady, her breaths even, though her calm was in shattered pieces. "I have to be on my way," she said. "I need to search the cemetery."

Glancing out at the street, Guy said, "Would you like me to come with you?"

She paused. A heavy silence hung between them, weighted by the occurrences of last night, until Catherine set a gloved hand on the table and said, "Thank you kindly, Mr. Nolan. I'd much appreciate your help."

He went down the hall to let Owen know, and Catherine went downstairs, waiting in the dim of the shop. The lamppost just outside had been lit; its brightness shone through the front window, light gleaming over the polished counter, to the clocks on the wall, reflecting off their glass casings.

The old staircase creaked and popped under Guy's footsteps.

He fetched a lantern from the back room and took his coat and hat from their place on the rack.

"How was your visit with Mr. Mallory?" Catherine asked as they headed out. "You didn't . . . you didn't tell him about Mr. Smith, did you?"

"No, no." Guy adjusted his grip on the unlit lantern, locking the door behind them. He offered her his arm as they started down the street. "I *did* ask him if anyone at the university might know something more of this timepiece, aside from the rumors, but—" He stopped, very abruptly, pressing his lips thin.

"Yes, Mr. Nolan?"

"Nothing." Then, in an entirely different tone, he said, "Have you supposed this timepiece may not be a pocket watch? It's not definite, is it? Perhaps it's a great long-case clock hidden in that old church."

"I've no idea how I'd carry that back to Mr. Ainsworth."

Guy smiled. "That would be quite the challenge."

The grounds of the public cemetery stretched out before them. Tall columns supported the stone arch above the front gates, the wrought-iron fence edging the sidewalk. Stone walls ran along the sides of the yard, the graves dark and damp from the afternoon's rain. Buildings lined the street bordering the back of the grounds. They were pressed close, old sandstone and white windows, smoke rising from their chimney tops.

They passed through the open gates and headed down a pathway marked with puddles turned to mud. Catherine already despaired the state of her skirts, her boots spattered with mire.

Guy made a sound of dismay as he stepped out of a puddle. "And these are my good trousers." He looked ahead of them. "Where do you want to start?"

There were rows upon rows of gravestones, the winding dirt

trails between them, the old mausoleums, the ruins of the church. Catherine hadn't any directions now, and finding the timepiece somewhere in such an expanse seemed at once an impossible task.

"I suppose," she said, "we can start at Mr. Smith's grave."

They found the plot with little trouble. Catherine surveyed the freshly turned earth, the loose clumps of grass, wondering how many others had been buried without markers to indicate their place.

"The timepiece ought to be around here, oughtn't it?" She turned to Guy. "Its magic worked on Mr. Smith. It should be close."

Guy studied the ground. Crouching down, he pressed one hand to the dirt. "It may not be in a grave, but it could be buried all the same. If it was left here years ago, it could be under soil and tree roots by now." He stood up and glanced toward the nearby willow tree. "Or perhaps in a hollow, if the piece is small enough."

They found no hollow in the willow, but there was one at the base of an oak tree some paces away. They sat down before it, staring into the dark space.

Guy lit his lantern, the flare of brightness illuminating the cracks in the bark, the dried and curling leaves about the trunk. The light reflected in Guy's eyes as he set down the lantern, peering into the hollow. Catherine reached a hand inside, but all she felt were cobwebs, undergrowth, and more dead leaves.

With a sigh, she removed her hand, wiping it on the grass. "If it's in a hollow, it's not this one."

They moved on, inspecting other trees, walking around the tall mausoleums with their padlocked bronze doors. The light faded as they continued along the cemetery paths, the air turning brittle and biting. It was well into evening, and unease tightened Catherine's chest, her heart thudding as she took note of the darkening sky. There seemed to be no one about the cemetery apart from them, its emptiness made glaring by the lengthening shadows, gusts of wind scraping the branches above their heads.

She said, "Mr. Nolan," and looked around to find he'd paused in front of a tombstone. His expression was solemn as he regarded it, his lantern held loosely at his side. When she said his name again, he glanced up, meeting her gaze.

"We'd best have a look in the church," she told him.

He nodded. Together, they started for the stone heap. In another corner of the cemetery, there lay the small windowed structure of the new watch house, a lookout post where people could watch over the dead, guarding them against resurrection men. As they neared it, Guy stopped, raising his lantern. He said, "There's someone over there."

Catherine spotted the figure: a man with a lantern of his own, coming around the side of the watch house. She swallowed. "Put out your light," she murmured.

Guy hurried to do so, speaking low and fast as the flame went out. "Should we not be here? It's quite late, isn't it?"

Few people wandered the city's cemeteries in the dark. Those who did were usually watchmen or grave robbers, and Catherine did not think this man was the latter. Before she could answer Guy, the stranger looked their way. He lifted his light, calling out, "Hello! Who's there?"

Catherine stood frozen for only a moment longer. Catching hold of Guy's sleeve, she said, "Mr. Nolan, *run*."

They ran, stumbling, slipping on the wet ground. The entrance was too far; Catherine darted onto the grass, her fear razor-sharp and clawing at the back of her throat. "Here," she gasped. "This way." She passed a tall cross marker and ducked beneath a low wall facing one of the older tombs. Guy came around after her, crouching down. They sat with their backs against the cool and grimy stone, catching their breaths.

Guy whispered, "I thought the watchmen only patrolled the private cemetery."

"More regularly, perhaps, but I've seen them make rounds here before." She looked over at him. He had his knees to his chest, his arms around them, his eyes shut tightly.

"Last spring," he said in a hushed tone. "Last spring, Miss Daly, they imprisoned three grave robbers." He swallowed, turning to meet her gaze. "They were flogged, and Sydney told me one of them died some days later from—from the wounds."

"We haven't robbed any graves," Catherine whispered back.

"We've taken poor Mr. Smith from his resting place," said Guy. He shuddered and reached over his shoulder, touching his back as if he were already imagining the lashing.

Catherine tried to quiet her breathing, tried to listen for the sound of footsteps past the roaring of blood in her ears. A flicker of light touched the tombstone, the words engraved there illuminated in the glow. She looked up, wide-eyed. The watchman set his lantern on the wall and took Guy roughly by the collar.

"You think you can hide from me, boy? I saw you run off." He yanked him to his feet and shoved an old pistol under his chin. "What are you doing here at this hour?"

Catherine scrambled up. "Sir," she said. "Please, let him alone. We've done nothing wrong."

Next to her, Guy stood completely still. His face was blank, white shock, his eyes black as the night sky.

The man glanced at Catherine. There was a hard glint in his eyes, the lantern light leaving half his face in shadow. Looking back at Guy, he pushed the barrel against his skin. "Answer me." The man studied him, eyes narrowed. Then his expression changed. "Wait. I know your face. You're Henry Nolan's son, aren't you?"

Guy stared back, wordless, as though he'd forgotten his own name. "Yes," he choked out finally. His voice wavered, and his breath caught. Tears slid down his face when he blinked. "I'm Guy. Guy Nolan."

"All right." The man tucked away his pistol. "Your father did me a good turn a few years back. My apologies if I gave you a fright."

Catherine exhaled in relief. Guy put a hand against the stone wall, wiping at his eyes with the other. "A fright," he echoed.

"You oughtn't be wandering through here this late," the man continued. "I won't tell your father, but have a care, eh?"

Guy didn't answer. The watchman looked from him to Catherine. He nodded at her. "Sorry for the trouble, miss. Good night."

He started back for the path. Catherine watched him go until he was out of sight. Then there were only the old graves, the cold night wind, and Guy Nolan shivering beside her. Softly, she said, "Are you all right, Mr. Nolan?"

He nodded without meeting her gaze. He picked up his lantern, tried to light it, but his hands were trembling and he couldn't manage it. Catherine took the matches from him. She lit the lantern and carried it as they made their way out of the cemetery.

Halfway to the watchmaker's shop, Guy stopped to be sick in an alleyway. And by the time they reached the flat, he was shaking even worse than he was when they were among the tombs. Catherine looked on as he slopped water over the edge of the washbowl in the kitchen. The chill from outside had settled into her bones; she tasked herself with building the fire—brushing out the grate, taking logs from the basket. Guy left briefly to go down the hall to his room. When he returned, he was in clean clothes, and Catherine had moved on to making tea, the fire burning strong in the hearth.

"Thank you," Guy said upon seeing it. They were the first words he'd said in a while, and his voice came out rough. His eyes were red-rimmed, his gaze shifting about the room.

Catherine brought the teapot to the table, set out saucers and cups. "I don't mind."

They sat across from each other, and Guy stared down at his hands.

"Mr. Nolan," Catherine said after a pause. "Is your father in? Should I wake him?"

"No." Guy looked up. He gave a quick shake of his head. "Thank you, Miss Daly, but I'm perfectly fine. I—I'm just . . . I haven't even a scratch on me." His mouth twisted, and he put his face in his hands, choking on a sob. "I've just never been so scared in all my life," he cried. "I thought he was going to kill me."

Catherine's heart ached. She reached out, her hand poised just over his shoulder. She wanted to comfort him somehow but knew not what comfort she could offer. In the end she pulled back, took up the teapot, and poured tea into their cups. She slid the saucer to him across the scrubbed table.

Downstairs, clocks chimed the hour. The sound was muffled, ringing up through the floorboards. Guy sniffed and wiped his face with a handkerchief. "Thank you," he said again, taking hold of his teacup.

Catherine drank her tea. "Do you know what he meant?" she asked. "The watchman? He—he said your father did him a good turn."

Guy hunched his shoulders. Curling his hands around his

cup, he said, "I suppose my father sold him some hours. It's what people are always thanking him for."

"Why did he stop?"

Guy looked to the fireplace, and Catherine followed his gaze. The wood in the grate crackled, turning to ash. The clock on the mantelpiece, as well as the darkness beyond the window glass, told her of the late hour.

Guy said, "I asked him to." He placed his cup neatly in its saucer. "The magic you use for the farewell service—it takes something from you, does it not?"

She shifted in her chair. "Time," she answered. "Time off my life."

His eyes widened a little. "Truly?"

"Yes. But the people we bring back don't return as Mr. Smith did. They're still dead." She ran a finger over the rim of her empty teacup. "They're—they're like ghosts, Mr. Nolan."

He leaned forward, holding her gaze. His eyes shone to a dark polish. "Our magic takes memories. My father would put pieces of time in a watch—an hour, more than an hour—and an equal amount of time would be forgotten from his past." He set his jaw. "The magic was eating away at him—I could see it. And he has dreadful nightmares sometimes."

A log tumbled in the hearth, but neither of them moved to fetch the poker.

"Other watchmakers in the city aren't keen on doing such business," Guy went on. "My father made quite a tidy profit. Once he stopped, well . . . a lot of clients didn't come back after that." He twisted his hands atop the table. "He doesn't wish me to use magic, and I agree, but now . . ."

Standing up, he headed over to the fireplace. He took the poker and tended to the fire, the flames flickering and curling about the wood. "Sydney Mallory doesn't do things for nothing," he told her. "If he's going to ask around about the timepiece, he wants a favor in return."

Catherine asked, "What sort of favor?" But she could already guess.

"He wants me to still time for him during resurrections—to avoid the watchmen." Guy turned to face her. "I've never done it before, Miss Daly. Magic." He held the poker limply at his side; for a moment, he looked dreamlike, fey, a knight with a fallen sword.

Catherine looked away. Closing her eyes, she listened to the tick of the mantel clock, the crackling of the fire. "I understand," she said. "It's all right. If you don't want to—I understand."

"No," said Guy. "I'll do it. I've already quite made up my mind."

She looked back around. He set down the poker, walking over to place his hands on the table. His eyes were dark and bright, his face flushed after being near the heat of the flames. "This is what I'm trying to tell you, Miss Daly. Honestly, I have little choice in the matter. I can suspend time for Sydney and he'll give me a cut of his pay, or I can do as my father did and start selling time to people. We're—we're going to lose the shop otherwise. Perhaps not next week or next month, but if things keep on the way they have—" He stopped, stepped back. He squeezed his eyes shut and pinched the bridge of his nose between forefinger and thumb. "Forgive me. I shouldn't have . . . I shouldn't have said all that."

Catherine stared at him. She felt a rush of sympathy so fierce it hurt her heart. She rose from her chair and clasped her hands in front of her. "It's been a long day," she said. "You ought to get some rest, Mr. Nolan."

"What about you?" He studied her face. "The timepiece—"

"I need to speak with my foreman. Mr. Ainsworth may have given me more time to search." She hoped for that, at least. Perhaps Spencer had managed to convince him of the fact she had no knowledge of the timepiece's whereabouts.

Guy accompanied her down to the shop. Gazing out the front window, he said, "Thank you again, Miss Daly. For earlier."

She finished tying her bonnet and looked up at his face. "You're welcome."

"Tomorrow—let me know what the word is, either way. I'll help however I can."

She nodded. "Good night, Mr. Nolan."

"Good night."

She made her way through the dimly lit streets back to the *Chronicle*. Inside, she breathed in the smell of metal and ink, surveying the empty floor. It felt like an age since she'd last been here.

Up on the third floor, she went to Spencer's room and tapped her knuckles lightly against the door. There was a part of her that didn't want him to answer, to have this night go on, and in the morning, everything to be as it was.

Spencer opened the door. He was in his nightclothes, but something about his face, the sharpness of his gaze, told her he hadn't been asleep. "Catherine." His voice was half a whisper. "Where have you been?"

Rather than answer, she asked, "Did you speak with him?"

"Yes." He paused. In that silence, Catherine knew she wouldn't like whatever he said next, but she willed her expression to keep from showing it. "Catherine, you should pack up. You oughtn't be here when he comes in tomorrow."

She fixed her eyes on the hall wallpaper. "What—what did he say?"

"Just what you already told me. He didn't take kindly to me

arguing the point, but here's some luck for you—he's having a meeting with Mr. Boyd tomorrow. I imagine he'll be too distracted to think on much else."

Mr. Boyd was the proprietor of the new paper in the city, the *Journal*.

Catherine picked at a curling seam in the wallpaper. It was below the gas light, and the stain there dirtied her fingertips. "What sort of meeting?"

"I don't know." Spencer rubbed at the skin between his eyebrows, as if attempting to push back a headache. "I heard some people say Mr. Boyd wants to buy the paper from him—or a share of it. I don't know," he said again.

"Right." She dropped her hand from the wall. "Well, I'm going to bed, then. I doubt I'll see you in the morning."

"Catherine, I'm sorry." He put a hand on the doorknob. She thought, oddly, for an instant, he was going to swing the door shut in her face. Instead, he bit down on his lip and added, "Just . . . keep away for a while. This will sort itself out, I'm sure."

A little ways down the hall, she turned back. "Thank you for trying, Spencer." She held his gaze in the dim. "Don't think this was your fault."

In her own room, she closed the door behind her, and across the small space, Bridget didn't stir from sleep. Catherine's eyes adjusted to the darkness; she washed up with water from the ewer and slipped on her nightgown. As she got into bed, her foot hit the box beneath it, the letters from her family tucked inside. She'd have to remember to pack those in her trunk. Pulling up the blankets, she turned to face the wall, listening to the muffled sounds of the city beyond the window.

It was a long time before she fell asleep.

CHAPTER THIRTEEN

CATHERINE STOPPED at the corner before the watchmaker's shop. It was a gray morning, a fine mist hanging in the air; she wore her coat and bonnet, her grip tight around her battered trunk. From here, she could see the green shopfront. A carriage rolled past, momentarily obscuring her view.

She made a start down the street. As she neared, the kitchen curtain twitched, the window was pushed open, and Guy Nolan leaned out of it.

"Hello, Miss Daly!"

Her heart thrilled, warmed, at the gladness in his voice.

She said, "Good morning, Mr. Nolan."

He folded his arms over the sill. Tipping his head to the side, he regarded her with a slight smile. The cuffs of his shirt were unfastened, his cravat loose about his neck. Then he appeared to take note of the trunk she carried, and his smile fell away. "My father's in the shop," he told her. "I'll be down in a minute." He ducked back inside, sliding the window closed.

She walked into the shop to find Henry Nolan behind the counter, cloth in hand, polishing one of the many clocks on the wall. He paused to look in her direction. "Good morning, Miss Daly. It is Miss Daly, isn't it? I heard Guy upstairs."

"Yes. Good morning, Mr. Nolan."

Like Guy, Henry wore spectacles. He took them off, put them in his trouser pocket, and set his cloth on the counter. There was a marked resemblance between father and son. They had the same fall of dark hair, the same angular features, though Henry's eyes were blue, not brown, with fine lines at the corners of them, his hair graying at the temples.

Just then, Guy came down the back staircase. He looked more put together than he had at the window, his cravat tied and centered. "Father," he said, "might I have a moment to speak with Miss Daly?"

Henry glanced over, meeting his gaze. "Very well." He went into the back room without closing the door, so Catherine still saw him at the desk, opening a drawer in search of something.

Guy turned to her. Keeping his voice low, he said, "Why do you have that trunk with you?"

"I need somewhere safe to put it." She adjusted her grip, holding the trunk out to him. "I can't go back to the newspaper at the moment, and I thought—I wondered if I might keep it here? For now?"

"Of course." Guy blinked, looked down, and took the luggage in his arms. "It'll be quite safe here. I'll store it upstairs."

"Thank you."

When he returned, they stood together at the front window,

whispering. The glass was fogged, streaked with condensation. The street beyond it was a hazy impression of watery sunlight and brown buildings; the people passing by were made into shadows, black cloaks flapping in the wind like raven wings.

Catherine asked, "Where is Mr. Smith?"

"Fernhill Park. At least, I hope so. I had to bring him there earlier, before my father woke up." Guy tugged a little at his cravat. "Will you wait for me? I can be out of here in fifteen minutes or so."

Waiting on the corner, she watched coaches rattle past, horses stamping their hooves, people heading in and out of shops along the street. The door to the watchmaker's shop opened, and Guy stepped out in his dark coat and hat. He glanced at his pocket watch before tucking it away, then looked up, caught sight of her, and made his way over.

"What's happened, then?" he asked.

Catherine told him the whole of it. Altogether, there wasn't much to tell. Without the timepiece, she couldn't return to the *Chronicle*. Without the timepiece, she was without a job.

"Oh, Miss Daly," Guy said in sympathy. "If you need somewhere to stop tonight, you're more than welcome back at our place."

She was rather hoping she might find the timepiece by tonight. Yet the more she thought on it, the more distant the possibility seemed to her.

"That's kind of you, Mr. Nolan."

Patting his coat pocket, he said, "I've a note to drop off for Sydney about this business. He'll ask around at the university." They paused at the sidewalk's edge, waiting for a gap in the traffic. "There's also a watchmaker across town who's a friend of my father's. He may know something. We could visit him, if you'd like. Someone made this timepiece, after all."

Catherine looked over. "That seems a fine idea."

He grinned.

After crossing the street, she added, "I'd like to go back to the cemetery, too."

"Oh." Guy hesitated. "Yes. Of course."

She recalled last night: how they'd run through the dark, the flash of the watchman's light, the terror in Guy's expression as the man took him by the collar and pressed a gun to his skin.

"It'll be quite safe in the day," she went on. "I can manage perfectly well on my own. And I doubt Mr. Smith is interested in going back."

"I see your point," said Guy. His relief was evident in his tone. "I was—I thought I might bring him to the tailor's today."

They came to Fernhill Park, a stretch of green space lined with walking paths, a wooden footbridge built across the pond. In the summer, the grass was shaded over by the canopies of oak and ash trees. Now the branches were almost bare of leaves, stark against the gray sky. Owen Smith sat on one of the park benches, tearing up pieces of bread and feeding the birds gathered on the path.

Guy narrowed his eyes. "Mr. Smith," he said slowly, "is that your breakfast?"

Owen tossed what remained in his hand to the birds. "Only some of it." He turned to them, shrugging his shoulders. "I'm not very hungry."

"Oh, for goodness' sake." Guy stepped up to the bench, sending the flock scattering in his wake. "Right. On your feet. We've a lot to do today."

Owen stood and brought one hand up to cover a yawn. He said, "Morning, Miss Daly," before fetching his hat off the bench and putting it on.

"Good morning, Mr. Smith."

They left the park together, Guy walking a little ahead. Catherine quickened her pace to fall in step with him. "Mr. Nolan," she said, "I can't see it being much longer before your father notices Mr. Smith. You can't leave him in the park all day. It's cold enough as is. What about in the winter?"

Rubbing his eyes, Guy said, "By then, he'll hopefully be apprenticed somewhere. I'll speak to my father about letting him stay if it comes to that. I know my father—he won't turn him away. But for now . . . Perhaps I am being fretful, but I don't want my father to worry, and Mr. Smith hasn't any money, nor anywhere else to go." He glanced over his shoulder and called to Owen, "Come along, Mr. Smith."

Owen was trailing some distance behind them, gazing out at the stretch of grass. He looked around and hurried to catch up. As he did, Guy turned back to Catherine. "Shall we meet in the afternoon? We can head over to the watchmaker's then. That is," he added with a smile, "if you don't find the timepiece in the cemetery." Owen came up on the other side of him. "Mr. Smith, I know a fine tailor. Why don't we pay him a call today? Miss Daly will be heading back to the cemetery for another search."

Owen looked between the two of them. "Miss Daly," he said, "Mr. Nolan told me what happened last night. Frightful business. Are you quite certain you want to go back?"

It was a matter of need rather than want, Catherine thought. She hadn't a chance of getting her job back without the timepiece in hand, and what evidence she had of its whereabouts traced back to the cemetery grounds.

"I'll be just fine," she told Owen.

"I've a stop to make at the lodging house first," Guy said. "If you want to walk with us a little ways."

• • •

Catherine knew the lodging house on Navy Street. It was adjacent to the river, near the docks, the proximity made noticeable by the heavy smell of silt, the creak and clank of ships at port, and dock workers calling out to one another. The house was almost as large as the print shop, four stories tall, the bricks water-stained and soot-marked.

Guy took an envelope from his coat and knocked on the door; Catherine and Owen looked on as an elderly woman answered. Guy doffed his hat. The two exchanged a few words, and Guy handed her the message he'd written for Sydney Mallory.

Once she closed the door, Guy headed back over to them. They had almost reached the corner when Owen glanced back at the lodging house. "What does Mr. Mallory do?" he inquired.

Guy grimaced. There was a pause in which Catherine thought he wouldn't answer, but the moment passed and he replied, "Unpleasant work."

"I daresay my work at that coffin shop was unpleasant." But Owen said it pleasantly. His expression changed, however, turned solemn, and he fell silent as they walked on.

At the next street, they parted ways, Catherine starting off in the direction of the cemetery. She hesitated at the front gates, looking over the graves still shrouded in morning fog. The sounds of the city quieted, grew distant, as she headed inside. She became more aware of her own footfalls, her breath misting in front of her. She walked down a trail they had taken yesterday, pausing when her eyes caught on a familiar name within a row of tombstones. It was the grave marker Guy had stopped at the night before. Now she realized why.

The name NOLAN was carved across the top, and below it, three names. The years of birth were different, but they had all died the same year—more than a decade ago.

Catherine tore her gaze away and continued along the path.

Guy hadn't mentioned having family buried here, and looking upon the grave felt like prying into his past.

She headed to the back of the cemetery, to the watch house. It was unmanned at this early hour, and she peered in through a window, considering the bare room. There was nothing to see but dirt tracked across the floor.

Instead, she turned her attention to the church. In the watery daylight, it appeared no less imposing, the empty bell tower rising up out of the fog. The stonework was dark and damp-stained like many of the graves, eroded by weather and time. When she came to the entrance, she noticed two women in mourning dress walking between the rows of graves.

"Oh, miss," said one of them. "I wouldn't venture in there. It's not safe."

Catherine stepped back from the doorway, heat rushing to her face. "Undoubtedly." She swallowed. "Good day."

Mud squished beneath her boots as she made her way around the other side of the ruins. She waited, leaning against the stone. Once the pair had moved on, she went back to study the front of the church. From a glance, it was clear she'd need a lantern. Shadows obscured much of the space, and debris littered the ground. Perhaps she could borrow one from Guy.

The city clock tolled the hour as she headed out of the cemetery. At the watchmaker's, it seemed Guy and Owen had yet to return from the tailor's. The back-room door swung open, and Henry Nolan took off his glasses to regard her. "Hello again, Miss Daly." His brow furrowed. "Is Guy not with you?"

Catherine crossed the shop floor, pausing at the counter. "He should be along in a moment. He asked me to meet him here."

The clocks on the wall ticked steadily, pendulums oscillating. Last night, Guy had told her his father no longer used magic, no longer sold hours. The timepiece she sought was of a different enchantment, but it was possible Henry might know something of it.

She said, "May I ask you something, sir?" And when he nodded, she went on. "I'm looking for a timepiece, an enchanted one. It—it's said to be able to bring back the dead."

Henry frowned. "I've heard of it, yes."

"What have you heard?"

He let out a sigh. Not unkindly, he said, "Only of its existence, Miss Daly. I imagine my son has mentioned to you that I don't enchant timepieces anymore. And the magic in that timepiece isn't magic I'm capable of doing."

Catherine inclined her head.

"If you don't mind my asking, why are you looking for such a thing?"

The words put an unexpected ache in her chest. He'd asked so carefully, so gently; if he were her father, she would've told him. But he wasn't. Her parents were miles from here, unknowing of her predicament. She'd lived in this city for two years, yet she felt more alone than she had that first night she'd spent at the print shop, with the memory of Father riding off on the cart sharp in her mind. She hadn't cried then, but she'd come close, and she felt close to tears now, standing before Henry Nolan in the small and tidy watchmaker's shop.

The bell above the shop door chimed, and Guy stepped in. He took off his hat but kept near the door, as though preparing for an imminent departure.

"Hello, Miss Daly," he greeted her cheerfully. "Hello, Father."

Catherine scrubbed hastily at her eyes. Bidding goodbye to Henry, she joined Guy at the door. He followed her outside, and on the street, she looked about for Owen.

"He's just around the corner," Guy told her, "at Mr. Fields's shop. He wanted to inquire about an apprenticeship, I believe."

She met his gaze. "What did you write to Mr. Mallory?"

Guy looked back at her. He held his hat at his side, and his brow creased with concern. "You didn't find it in the cemetery, then?"

"Not as of yet."

"Ah, well." He replaced his hat, offering her his arm as they started down the pavement. "I agreed to the arrangement. I told him to meet us at the shop if anything turns up."

"And this friend of your father's—do you really suppose he'll know something of the timepiece?"

"I'm not certain what Mr. Everley knows, but there's no harm in asking, is there?"

His optimism did little to cheer her. She was still lost in memories, the past shadowing her thoughts. It'd been her decision to come here after her brother left home. A purely sensible choice—before she'd learned to set type and organize sorts, before she'd become familiar with the creaks and groans of the building settling at night and the way sunlight patterned the wallpaper of her room in the mornings.

Everything she relied upon in life was slipping between her fingers, falling away, too quickly for her to grasp.

"Miss Daly?" said Guy.

Just ahead, the wooden sign above the cordwainer's door swayed in the wind. Owen Smith stood with his back to the shop, his hands in his coat pockets. He looked out at the passing carriages with a downheartedness that Catherine herself felt all too keenly.

"I don't know what I'll do," she murmured, "if I don't find it."

Guy gave her a reassuring smile. "We may yet uncover something," he said. "By tonight, we could have our answers."

CHAPTER FOURTEEN

MR. EVERLEY'S SHOP lay in another part of Old Town, so it was rather a long walk there. Catherine's teeth chattered, her toes numbing in her boots. They headed down a narrow street, where a mossy stone wall edged one side of the pavement. The buildings were built of the same gray stone, the shopfronts along the way painted an assortment of colors. It wasn't an area of the city Catherine was well acquainted with, and it was a good deal quieter, away from the river, from the market stalls.

A fierce gust of wind nearly carried off Guy's hat. He caught hold of it and said, "Oh dear."

"We're not lost, are we?" asked Owen.

"Not lost," Guy said firmly. "But perhaps we should've taken an omnibus. I haven't visited in some time—I forgot just how far it is."

Catherine said, "How well do you know him? Mr. Everley?"

"I've known him almost my whole life. He and my father have been friends since I was a child."

They came upon the shop a little while later. Above the door, in white paint, it read EVERLEY—HOROLOGIST. There were clocks on display in the front window, golden and gleaming, in engraved dark wood cases. Inside, the place was arranged in a similar fashion to the Nolans' shop. The countertop was just as clean and polished, the wallpaper a shade darker, but clocks still took up much of it. Catherine rubbed her gloved hands together, grateful to be out of the wind. She wondered if Everley had the same magic as the Nolans, if he too once sold hours to people.

There was a set of stairs near the entrance—the newel post faded and scuffed, the steps dipped in the middle—and Guy stopped at the foot of it, calling up, "Hello? Mr. Everley?"

Above them, the floorboards creaked under footsteps. And someone replied, "Guy?" A man descended the stairs, neatly dressed in a white shirt and black silk waistcoat, a frock coat and gray trousers. He looked about the same age as Henry Nolan, his black hair threaded with silver. He smiled. "It's good to see you. What brings you here?"

Guy smiled back. "Good afternoon, sir."

The man glanced from Guy to Catherine and Owen. His brow creased. "Is your father not with you?" he asked.

"He's back at the shop. These are my friends Miss Daly and Mr. Smith," Guy added, gesturing to them. "Miss Daly, Mr. Smith, this is Mr. Everley."

Catherine said politely, "How do you do, sir?"

"We're needing information about a particular timepiece," Guy told him.

"Well, come upstairs. I'll build up a fire."

In the kitchen, Everley swept the fireplace clean and put coal into the grate. Catherine sat beside Owen at the table, while Guy remained standing near the hearth. Books crowded the mantelpiece, a shelf clock placed in the center. A mirror hung on the wall above, and Catherine saw Guy's reflection in the glass. He'd removed his overcoat, hat, and gloves, and his hair was a little disheveled, his cheeks still pink from the chill outside.

"Is Mrs. Everley not in?" he asked.

"No. She's out of town at the moment, visiting her sister." Everley returned his poker to the rack of other fireplace tools, moving toward the kitchen counter. "And how is your father? Is he well?"

"Very well," Guy said with alacrity. He took a seat at the table across from Catherine, and the worries he'd expressed to her last night felt like well-buried secrets now.

Everley set out a plate of biscuits and poured tea for each of them. He sat down at the table, and when Guy turned the conversation to the timepiece, Everley replied, "You don't want any business with that. I'd leave it for those at the university to find, if they haven't already."

"It's my employer who wants it—at the *Chronicle*," Catherine told him. She swallowed, meeting his gaze. "He tasked me with finding it. Doing so is the only chance I have of keeping my job."

Everley let out a sigh, closing his eyes briefly. "No one ought to have it, to be using magic of that sort—"

"Have you heard tell of who might've made it?" asked Guy.

Everley paused. "No," he said. "But I don't suppose it's very old. I've only heard rumors of it in the past decade."

The device was thought to be buried in Owen's grave; it could've been crafted around the time of his death. Catherine glanced his way, but he kept his eyes trained on his teacup.

On their way out, Everley stopped Guy in the hall. Catherine hesitated around the corner at the top of the stairs, listening.

Everley said, "Does Henry know about this?"

"Sir?"

"Does he know you're searching for this timepiece?"

"Good gracious, no. I'm helping Miss Daly, is all."

There was a pause. Catherine looked to Owen, waiting on the landing just below.

"Mr. Everley." Guy lowered his voice. "You don't think I'd ever use it, do you?"

"No," said Everley softly. "I only fear your father might."

Guy answered in a rather stiff manner. "I don't believe so, sir."

"Guy . . ."

"Thank you for your help, Mr. Everley. We'll manage rightly."

At his approaching footsteps, Catherine started down to the shop floor. Through the window, the light was waning, and the clocks along the wall were turned to dark shapes, silhouettes, ticking on, as constant a sound as in the Nolans' shop.

Guy came downstairs, and Catherine turned to him. Raising her eyebrows, she asked, "Is everything all right?"

"Quite."

He helped her into her coat before pulling on his own. Owen took his coat from the rack and gazed out the window. "I didn't realize," he said, sounding thoughtful. "Are there . . . are there many people looking for this timepiece?"

They stepped outside, heading down the quiet street, and Catherine said, "Well, it is something many people want—magic to return the dead to life. One could bring back one's family, one's friends."

"But they don't know," said Owen. "If people are brought back without their memories . . ." He paused, biting his lip. "I wouldn't know my family even if they were standing right in front of me."

Catherine clucked her tongue. "Now, Mr. Smith, you don't know that for certain. Your memories could still come back."

Owen looked away from her. His eyes shone bright and clear as he fixed his gaze ahead of him. "Perhaps it's better if I don't remember. I've no idea what I was like, truly. I might've been an awful person."

"You're being too hard on yourself, Mr. Smith," Guy said. "I'm sure you were a perfectly decent fellow, just as you are now."

At that, Owen sighed, but he said nothing further. Catherine cast her eyes down to her boots, still muddied from her wanderings in the graveyard.

Owen's words about the timepiece gnawed at her. It was a flawed bit of magic, that was true, to bring a person back to life without any memory of who they were. She couldn't help thinking that perhaps the device ought not to be found—by her or anyone else. As Everley had said, no one should be using such magic.

At the watchmaker's, the OPEN sign was upon the door, though the shop was empty. The gas light flared as Guy turned up the lamps. He reached the back staircase, calling up, "Father!"

Catherine's gaze drifted to the back-room doorway. She started as a shadow moved near the worktable.

"Afternoon," said Sydney Mallory. He leaned against the door-frame, crossing his arms.

"What are you doing back there?" Guy asked.

"Your father said I might wait for you." He looked around at the three of them, considering, assessing. "He wasn't sure where you'd gone."

Something inside Catherine drew tight at his tone. There was an underlying sharpness to it, clear as a shard of glass. He was without his coat and hat, and she realized belatedly they were already hanging on the coatrack alongside theirs. They joined him in the back room, though there wasn't much in the way of space; Sydney sat on the chair behind the desk, Catherine and Owen on the sofa. Watchmaking tools crowded the desk's surface, shining under the light of an emerald-green shaded lamp. There were metal trays holding loose parts, tweezers, magnifying glasses, small pots of oil, other things Catherine couldn't identify. A silver pocket watch was set to one side—the glass over the dial cracked through the middle—together with half-melted candles and empty cups of tea.

Guy closed the door and remained standing. "Did you get my letter?" he asked.

"Yes," said Sydney. His gaze slid to Catherine, then Owen. He said nothing further.

"Well? Did you go to the university?"

"Indeed, I did."

"And?"

Sydney leaned back in his chair. "Why are you so interested in this timepiece, Guy? It's only a story, after all. Are you sure it even exists?" He returned his attention to Owen. "Are you still looking for work, Mr. Smith?"

"Yes," said Owen, though his voice rose a little, as if he were uncertain. "Do you . . . work at the university? Mr. Nolan said—"

Sydney interrupted him with a laugh. "Do I work at the university? Guy, you didn't tell him that, did you?"

Guy stood motionless by the door. Catherine supposed he'd rather steer past this conversation completely.

Still looking at Sydney, Owen wrung his hands together. "Mr. Nolan said your work was . . . unpleasant. If I may ask, what is it you do?"

A smile tugged at the edge of Sydney's mouth. His eyes glinted in the lamplight as he leaned forward. "Yes, I'll tell you, shall I? Perhaps you'll take to it as well. You can make quite a bit of coin, if you can stomach it."

Guy started, "Sydney—"

Sydney paid him no mind. "You see, Mr. Smith, I dig up bodies. Those learned men at the university? The anatomists? They need a ready supply for their dissections, more than just executed criminals, and they pay finely for them."

Owen blanched. He pressed back against the sofa cushions, staring at Sydney. He let out a quiet, shuddering breath, and the next moment, he was on his feet, stumbling out of the room, the door slamming shut behind him. Catherine heard the staircase creak sharply as he made his way up.

Guy shot Sydney a furious look. "Well done, Sydney. Are you pleased with yourself? You've just terrified him half to death."

"He asked. I've yet to find a delicate way to put it."

Guy folded his arms over his chest. "Do you have information about the timepiece or not? If not, you can leave."

Sydney drew himself up. He stood over Guy, looking down at him. Guy held his ground, chin tipped up, eyes narrowed.

"Why," Sydney began, "should I tell you anything when you've lied to me?"

"I haven't lied to you."

"No? You're not a good liar, Guy. I can see the shape of it." Sydney pointed at the door. "Is Mr. Smith staying here? He ought to be in a poorhouse if he can't find work. How do you even know him?" Rounding on Catherine, Sydney continued. "And you, Miss Daly—you're seeking this timepiece, yes?"

Catherine stood up. "Mr. Mallory, pardon my saying so, but I don't see how any of this is your business."

"You're asking for my help. That makes it my business." Sydney peered up at the ceiling before looking to Guy, his eyes alight with curiosity. "He was dead, wasn't he? Mr. Smith. I can't fathom why else he's here, all of a sudden, and you're so keen on finding this timepiece, all of a sudden. It's worked its magic on him."

Catherine drew in a breath. "Mr. Mallory—"

"You can't tell anyone, Sydney." Guy's voice took on a pleading edge. "He hasn't any memory of who he was."

Catherine said, "Mr. Ainsworth at the *Chronicle* is the one who wants the timepiece. He thought it was buried in Mr. Smith's plot."

Sydney raised an eyebrow. "And it wasn't?"

"No. But Mr. Smith returned to life, so it's likely somewhere near there."

"I see." Sydney pressed his knuckles to his mouth. He looked between the two of them. "Perhaps you ought to bring Mr. Smith to the university."

Guy bristled. "To the medical department? Why ever would we do that?"

"They'd want to see him, most assuredly," said Sydney with a smile. "It's a strange sort of magic that's brought him back."

"Well, it'll be his decision," Guy replied. "And I doubt very much he'll want to step foot there after you spoke of it so horrifically."

Sydney moved past him to the door, his smile widening. "Ask him. I'll stop by in the morning—he can give me his answer then." He set a hand on the doorknob. Turning back around, he added, "And there's to be a funeral tomorrow at the public cemetery. I'll need your services come nightfall."

"No," Guy snapped. "You haven't given us any information."

"For that, you may want to come along to the university." With a nod at Catherine, Sydney left the room, closing the door behind him.

The bell above the shop door chimed as he headed out.

Guy closed his eyes, releasing a sigh. "That didn't go as well as I'd hoped," he said.

Catherine looked away. It wasn't what she'd hoped for, either.

Guy opened the door, letting in more light, and positioned the chair Sydney had sat in so it was flush against the worktable. Reaching across it, he put out the lamp.

"Miss Daly." He glanced her way. "Shall we see where he's gone?"

He meant Owen. She couldn't hear anything from upstairs, the quiet broken only by the soft, collected ticking of the clocks in the next room. She nodded, and they started for the stairs together.

CHAPTER FIFTEEN

IN THE KITCHEN, they found Owen at the table across from Henry Nolan. A cup of tea sat steaming in front of him, but when he saw them, he stood abruptly. "Forgive me, Mr. Nolan," he said to Henry. "I'm afraid I must be on my way."

Guy stepped forward. "Mr. Smith—"

But Owen strode past them as if they were ghosts. He ducked his head and took to the stairs. Catherine called after him, "Mr. Smith, where are you going?"

He didn't answer.

Henry made his way over. The fire in the grate cast him in shadow and light, accentuating the lines at the corners of his eyes. "He seems rather upset."

"Sydney was unkind to him," Guy replied. Rubbing his forehead, he turned to his father. "What did he tell you?"

"Nothing of it—I could see it on his face. Is he a friend of yours? He said he's an apprentice at the coffin shop on Burnside Lane."

Catherine glanced to Owen's neglected teacup.

Oh, Mr. Smith.

Then Henry's attention settled on her. "Hello again, Miss Daly," he said lightly.

"Good afternoon, Mr. Nolan." She nodded to him even as her heart thudded with unease. She clasped her hands together in the hopes of steadying herself. "My apologies, but I must be getting back to the *Chronicle*." Giving Guy a pointed look, she added, "Mr. Nolan, if you might accompany me . . ."

"Of course, Miss Daly."

They turned for the door. Before they left, Henry said, "Come home directly, Guy."

Guy hesitated. He looked as if he were weighing his next words, but in the end he said only, "Yes, Father."

Outside the shop, the street was not as busy as it was earlier in the day. Few people were about, and fewer carriages. Catherine looked along the row of buildings on the other side of the street. Painted shopfronts, white sash windows.

"Where do you think he'd go?" she said, turning to Guy. "Shall we try the park?"

He nodded tightly.

When they came to it, they walked the same path they'd taken that morning. Tree branches shivered in the breeze, some leaves still clinging in place, autumn colors of yellow and red-brown. The pond across the green glinted in the evening light, fallen leaves circling its edges.

Owen Smith stood in the middle of the footbridge. His coat was the same dark gray as the water below, and he looked faded as a shadow, his shoulders hunched as he stared down into the murk.

Catherine said, "Mr. Smith, are you all right?"

He didn't look at either of them, but his mouth crooked down. He shook his head.

"Sydney shouldn't have spoken so carelessly," said Guy. "I should have—"

"Is it true?" Owen whispered. "He's a resurrectionist?"

Guy leaned against the bridge beside him. "Yes."

Owen swallowed hard, looking down at himself. "Would he have dug me up?"

"No." Guy glanced to Catherine. He cleared his throat. "No, Mr. Smith, you were—I mean, your body was rather . . . You had been dead for a long time. The anatomists—they need fresh corpses."

Owen scrubbed at his red-rimmed eyes with his coat sleeve.

Placing a gentle hand on his shoulder, Guy said, "My father is waiting for me, so I need to head back, but wait for me at the corner and I'll let you in." He looked around, meeting Catherine's gaze. "And you, Miss Daly."

He left the bridge, starting down the path, as the clock tower tolled the hour. Catherine watched him until he was a dark figure in the distance, just another gentleman passing through the park. She turned back to Owen.

"Mr. Mallory knows about your situation," she told him. "And about the timepiece. He thought you might consider visiting the university."

Owen folded his arms atop the parapet, peering over the bridge into the water. "What for?" His voice shook. "So they may cut me open and study my insides?"

"Mr. Smith," Catherine chided. "You're not a cadaver. Mr. Nolan and I won't let you come to harm."

He turned to her. There was still something raw about his

countenance, but he smiled a tiny, hesitant smile, and it brightened his whole face. "I'll go," he said. "If you and Mr. Nolan come along, I'll go."

"Very well, then." And Catherine smiled back at him.

It was fully dark by the time Guy led them inside the shop and put the CLOSED sign on the door. A couple of lamps were still lit along the wall, burning low in their brackets. Light reflected over the clock dials, the pendulums and weights, the polished cases. Guy took Catherine's coat and bonnet, hanging them up.

She studied his face in the dim. "Your father . . . ?"

"He's already asleep. He won't wake." He ran a hand through his hair and added, "He takes medicine to help with his nightmares. He'll sleep until morning."

Catherine couldn't help but glance up. She waited for some creak to alert her to the fact that Henry Nolan was indeed awake, but no footsteps sounded on the floorboards. There was only the low, occasional groan of the building settling, the temperature falling with the evening. She shivered.

"You may sleep on the sofa down here, Miss Daly," Guy continued. "I hope that's agreeable."

"Thank you, Mr. Nolan."

They headed upstairs, where Guy collected blankets for her from the linen chest, and Catherine fetched clothes from her trunk. After dinner, after Owen went off to bed, Guy took a seat in a wingback armchair by the fireplace. The floral-patterned upholstery was worn thin along the chair arms; the printed roses were faded to a pale pink. He'd loosened his cravat and unfastened his shirt cuffs. He tipped his head back, a certain light to his eyes as he looked over at the hearth. In the grate, the fire was slowly dying, the wood blackened, the coals glowing red.

Catherine clasped her hands in front of her. "Well," she said. "Good night, then."

She made to leave, and Guy said softly, "Wait."

Catherine glanced back at him.

He straightened up. "Are you . . . ? Are you very tired? Only I thought we might"—his face reddened, noticeable even in the low light—"sit together for a time. If you'd like."

She paused, eyebrows raised. She didn't think the pause to be more than a moment, but in that time Guy's blush turned a deeper scarlet, and he said, "No? Yes, as I thought. Good night, Miss Daly." He looked away, fixing his attention on the fireplace.

She went and sat down in the armchair opposite him. "I'm not very tired."

He leaned forward. A grin spread across his face. "Nor am I."

Taking up the poker, he nudged at the burnt logs, sending white flakes of ash into the air. He sighed and set it back down. As he did, his gaze flicked up to the painted miniature on the mantelpiece. "Miss Daly, I've been wondering." He looked over at her. "Your family . . . are they . . . ? Do you not have . . . ?"

Catherine swallowed against the sudden tightness in her throat. "I have a family."

"Oh. It's just—you've never mentioned them." He bit his lip and added anxiously, "I'm sorry. Am I being too familiar?"

"No." She shook her head. "No, it's only . . . They're out in the country. I came to the city to work at the *Chronicle*, and I haven't been home in the two years since."

Guy tilted his head. The fading light of the fire played across his cheek, the curve of his jaw. "You must miss them."

"Yes. Terribly, sometimes. I write almost every week." She looked to the mantel clock, watching the slow movement of the minute hand. "My older brother, John, is often away from home too. He works in the mines. And there's my younger sister, Anne. She'll be fourteen now." She could see their faces in her mind's eye as clearly as the framed painting beside the clock.

"I had two older brothers," said Guy. He nodded to the painting. "That's Robert. He was the eldest. Then Wilfrid, but we haven't any pictures of him. They passed away from fever along with my mother when I was small."

Catherine murmured, "I'm sorry." She'd printed death notices for whole families struck down by fateful accidents or disease. It was not an uncommon plight, but that didn't make it any less sorrowful.

"Thank you. I can't really remember them." He leaned back in his chair. "My father and I get on well. Everything I know about our trade, I learned from him."

The last of the flames flickered out, leaving them in near darkness. Behind Guy's chair, light from the street shone in through the window, the pattern of the lace curtains casting a shadow over the far wall.

Something about the encroaching night made Catherine quiet her voice to a whisper. "Do you think we'll find something out at the university?"

"Sydney seems certain," Guy replied. "And I suppose they do have more knowledge at their disposal."

"But no one there has found it." Catherine twisted her hands in her lap. "What if . . . ? What if Mr. Smith was murdered for it?"

Guy's eyebrows went up. "Do you think it belonged to him?"

"Why else would it be said to be buried in his grave?"

Looking toward the kitchen doorway, Guy frowned. "We won't know, will we? He doesn't remember anything of it."

Catherine stood up and smoothed out her skirts. "We ought to get some sleep," she said. "We shan't be getting much tomorrow night if we're going to the cemetery."

"You're quite right, Miss Daly." He tipped his head back against the chair, his smile soft with sleepiness. "And we'll have to wake early, before my father does." He rubbed at his eyes, getting up. "I'll fetch you a candle."

"Thank you."

He pottered around the kitchen in the dim, finding matches and a candlestick holder. The back of his waistcoat was creased, his hair sticking up in parts. Below them, the clocks chimed the hour, tones low and recurring.

Guy passed her the candle. Their fingers brushed, and he drew back quickly, a blush rising in his cheeks. He said, "Be careful on the stairs."

"Yes." She swallowed. "Good night, Mr. Nolan."

"Good night, Miss Daly."

She made her way by candlelight down to the shop floor. As she slipped into the back room, putting the candle on the table, she smiled to herself. Despite the fact that it was her first night away from the print shop in two years, despite the fact that she may no longer have a job there, she felt a certain steadiness.

She could possibly discover the timepiece tomorrow. In the meanwhile, she was safe, here under this roof, with her family's letters and her belongings from home packed away in her trunk. She liked the reliable ticking of the clocks, the comfortable sofa, the wash of pink she'd seen across Guy's cheeks as he'd bade her good night.

Settling beneath the blankets, she fell into dreamless sleep.

CHAPTER SIXTEEN

CATHERINE WOKE NEAR dawn. When she headed up to the kitchen, she found Guy was already making breakfast, well dressed for the day. He wore a crisp white shirt, a dark-blue waistcoat, his trousers pressed and his boots polished.

"Good morning," he said upon seeing her. "I've woken Mr. Smith, so he should be joining us shortly." He set out plates and silverware, bread and butter and jam.

Catherine raised a hand to her hair, smoothing back the loose strands. She'd done it up in a neat chignon, and she'd donned a clean brown dress. Sitting at the table, she asked, "Did you sleep well?"

He glanced up, meeting her gaze with a smile. "Quite well. I hope you didn't mind the sofa."

"Not at all."

His eyes shifted to the doorway as Owen entered the room. "Mr.

Smith, there you are. Here, sit and eat something. We ought to be ready before Sydney gets here."

Beyond the window, the sky was deep blue, lightening with the coming dawn. They ate by lamplight, how Catherine had often eaten breakfast at the *Chronicle*. Guy fetched paper and pen to write a note to his father, left it on the counter, and opened a small tin, taking out a few coins. After putting on their coats and hats, they waited for Sydney Mallory near the front of the shop.

Clocks lined the window display—small brass carriage clocks with carrying handles, decorative mantel clocks. Guy busied himself winding those that needed winding, and though there was no dust to be seen, he retrieved a cloth from the back room and began polishing the display. Catherine looked on, sleepy-eyed, charmed by the care he took, the way he angled the clock faces toward the streetlight, studying each one.

She didn't catch sight of Sydney until he knocked on the door. When Guy answered it, Sydney looked over at Owen. "Are you set on visiting the university after all? Very good. I rather thought so."

They followed him out onto the street. The morning was bitter cold; Catherine's teeth chattered as they waited for a passing omnibus. Guy paid Owen's fare as well as his own; Catherine and Sydney followed after them, stepping up into the coach. At this early hour, there were scant few passengers. Catherine sat on the wooden bench next to Owen, Guy and Sydney sitting just across from them.

They started down the road, the coach wheels bumping over the cobbles. Guy removed his hat and fidgeted with the brim. His eyes cut to Sydney as the other boy leaned forward, hands clasped, his gaze steady on Owen.

"Guy tells me you don't remember aught before you died,"

he said, his voice quiet but clear. "Does that mean you don't remember dying?"

Owen frowned. "No," he said shortly.

Guy said, "Don't needle him, Sydney, *please*."

"I'm only curious." Still looking at Owen, Sydney leaned back in his seat. "What a shock it must've been for you—waking in a grave! I can't imagine."

Catherine turned toward Owen. "I think it would be wise," she started, "if you did not mention the entirety of what happened to you to those at the university."

He swallowed visibly. "I don't even know the entirety. Isn't that why we're going?"

"I agree with Miss Daly," said Guy. "We ought to think of some story—"

"Nonsense!" Sydney cut in. "No one there will care to see him if we don't tell them the truth of the matter."

The omnibus made another stop. They had reached a main street; outside the coach windows, shopkeepers were sweeping their front steps, arranging the merchandise in their displays. The omnibus moved on, turning a corner, and Catherine narrowed her eyes at Sydney. She asked, "Who are you bringing us to meet, Mr. Mallory?"

"One of the medical students. Francis Williams. He's a good sort."

Guy took out his glasses to polish them, but glanced up to share a smile with Catherine. He said, "He sounds remarkable."

Sydney snapped, "Oh, yes, Guy, because what you do is so adventurous. *Listen*. Francis is a fine fellow. If we tell him about Mr. Smith here, he'll keep quiet."

They came to the wide stretch of the river, and the omnibus rattled onto North Bridge, slowing amid the surrounding traffic.

The water below was black as an ink spill in the early-morning light, rowboats and barges navigating the harbor.

Once they reached the other side, more passengers stepped on and off. They passed the city library—smooth red sandstone, carvings in the shadows of the archways—and the marble columns of the museum. The peaked roofs rose higher than any in Old Town, where the tallest building was the clock tower in Elgin Square.

Near the hospital, the four of them got off the omnibus to walk the rest of the way to the university's medical department.

The building Sydney led them to was a great stone pile. In the courtyard before it, the grass lay pale and glittering with morning frost, crunching beneath their feet. A group of young men in wool overcoats stood outside the double doors, talking with one another. Catherine hoped they wouldn't question them, and though a few glanced over as they started up the steps, none of the men remarked on their presence.

Sydney ushered them inside, the doors opening onto a polished entrance of dark wood with a grand carpeted staircase, light from one of the high windows gilding the banister. Guy tilted his head back, and Catherine followed his gaze to the lit chandeliers between the wood beams spanning the ceiling.

"Francis has rooms here," said Sydney, heading for the stairs. "But I've never paid him a call this early in the day. He might be at a lecture."

Catherine asked, "Does he know anything of the timepiece?"

With a smile, Sydney replied, "I daresay he does. You'll have to ask him, won't you, Miss Daly?"

And yet, when they came to Francis's door on the fourth floor, no one answered.

"Well," said Sydney, sounding mildly irritated. "Perhaps we should try the library. It's back downstairs."

The library was at the far end of the building, an expansive room filled with bookshelves that soared up to the arched ceiling. Claw-foot tables lined the space, marble sculptures set against the stacks, their shadows stretching across the floorboards. Sydney surveyed the room from the doorway. Catherine looked about at the bent heads of those reading at the tables. The place was quiet, but not unnervingly so. It was like the print floor without the clatter of the presses, that same concentration to the task at hand.

Sydney started forward, peering between the stacks. He said, "Ah," and directed them to a table near one of the tall windows. A young man sat there alone, a book open in front of him, other leather-bound tomes piled at his elbow. His hair was wavy and blond, his waistcoat embroidered green silk. He glanced up, and Catherine saw his eyes were green as well—a shade paler than his waistcoat. His brow furrowed. "Sydney?" he said. "What . . . ?" Then, taking in the sight of Catherine, Guy, and Owen, he added, "Hello."

"Good morning, Francis," said Sydney. "We don't mean to disturb you at your studies, but we've a matter to discuss—one you ought to find quite interesting—if we might speak in private."

Francis smiled a little, gesturing at the empty table. "Isn't this private enough?"

"I'm afraid not."

Releasing a sigh, Francis said, "Very well. Give me a moment." He stood and took up the book he was reading, along with one other from the pile, holding them against his chest. "We'll go upstairs."

As they walked, Sydney made the introductions. "Francis Williams, this is Guy Nolan. His father is a watchmaker in Old Town. These are his friends Miss Daly and Mr. Smith."

Francis inclined his head. "Lovely to meet you."

Back at the entrance, Catherine slowed, pausing at the foot of the stairs.

Guy, noticing her hesitation, said, "Miss Daly?"

There was a man she recognized heading down the opposite corridor. He wore a dark frock coat, his light-brown hair slicked down and curled at the sides. She'd seen him a few times at the print shop, though he had no place there.

Mr. Boyd, proprietor of the *Journal*.

When Guy said her name again, she picked up her skirts and started after him.

On the fourth floor, Francis opened the door to his room. It was rather plainer than Catherine had expected. The arrangement was similar to her room at the print shop, though the furnishings were a fair bit nicer, and he had it to himself instead of having to share it with another student. A spray of flowers graced the windowsill, and everywhere else there lay books and papers, pens and inkpots.

Francis placed the books he carried on his desk. Turning around, he said, "What is it, then?"

Sydney opened his mouth, then closed it. His gaze flickered to Guy, to Catherine and Owen. "Perhaps you might explain," he said vaguely.

Catherine looked over at Francis. "We're searching for a timepiece."

"Oh, yes," he said. "Sydney mentioned that. In fact, someone else was here making inquiries about it just yesterday."

"What?" said Sydney. "Who?"

"A man from the *Invercarn Chronicle*, I believe. I didn't speak to him myself."

Catherine cast her eyes down, jaw clenched. Ainsworth. Ainsworth had been here. And if he was asking about the timepiece, did that mean he no longer thought she had it?

Guy asked, "What do you know of this timepiece, Mr. Williams?"

"I know it's powerful magic." Francis tapped his fingers against the edge of his desk. "It's not the sort of enchantment one could make on one's own, is it?"

"Do you have any knowledge of where it might be?"

"I mean . . ." Francis frowned, rubbing his chin. "Some fellows here think it's somewhere in the public cemetery, but there are others—others who say it's still with whoever made it, tucked away in a shop drawer or some such place. That seems the more likely possibility to me, at least. If it was in the cemetery, surely someone would've come across it by now." His gaze shifted from Guy to Sydney. "Is this all you wished to discuss? I've a lecture in"—he took out his pocket watch, checked the time—"less than half an hour."

Catherine looked to Owen, as did Guy and Sydney. He was quite pale, his grip tight around the hat in his hands. He gave a small shake of his head and fixed his attention on his boots.

Sydney narrowed his eyes. "Yes, Francis," he said. "Thank you."

"All right." Francis glanced out the narrow window above the desk, before starting back toward them, making for the door. "Will you be coming back tonight? Only, I already told Professor Blackwood you planned on it."

"Indeed. A little after midnight, I should think."

Francis walked with them back down to the entrance, bidding them farewell. Outside, they made their way across the courtyard. It was turning out to be a fine day despite the chill, sunlight reflecting off the windows of the stone buildings.

"I couldn't tell him," said Owen. His breath misted in the air. "Please, I—I just—"

"You needn't tell anyone you don't want to," Catherine replied.

"And we know more about the timepiece than he does," Guy put in. "It's as you said, Miss Daly—the timepiece must certainly be somewhere in that cemetery to have worked its magic as it did."

Catherine recalled the second night she and Guy had gone seeking the device, the gloom and stillness of the graveyard, and her attempt the next morning, standing before the church ruins shrouded in fog. Now Ainsworth was at the university, asking questions. Perhaps she could reason with him if he'd given up on the notion that she'd stolen it. She could return to her print work and continue the search.

"I'm going to go to the *Chronicle*," she said.

Guy looked her way.

"Mr. Ainsworth can't think I have the timepiece if he's asking after it here. He may let me have my job back."

Bringing a hand to his cravat, Guy tugged at the dark fabric. "Miss Daly," he said. "Are you sure?"

"Quite sure." Though what a terrible lie that was. She felt at once completely knotted and moments away from coming undone.

But even so, her mind was set.

CHAPTER SEVENTEEN

CATHERINE STOOD a little ways down the street from the print shop. After crossing the river, Sydney had headed in the direction of the lodging house, while Guy had brought Owen back to the watchmaker's, before coming along with Catherine. He paused beside her on the sidewalk now, looking over at the dark brick building.

"What shall I do," he asked, "if you don't come back out?"

"I'll be all right," Catherine told him. "And if not, I'm sure you'll think of something valiant, provide some distraction so that I might escape."

Guy's eyes flickered to hers. He glanced away just as quickly, swallowing hard. "Of course," he said. "A distraction."

"Fear not, Mr. Nolan." She offered him a reassuring smile. "I'll return directly. I only need to speak with Mr. Ainsworth for a moment."

With that, she continued on toward the shop. The building was soot-stained like every other in Old Town, the brass sign on the door weather-worn. Catherine let herself in and started across the print floor. The workday had begun; most people were at their desks and took no notice of her. Those who did simply nodded and smiled, and Catherine did her best to keep her expression pleasant. It seemed news had not spread about her predicament. Perhaps Ainsworth hadn't yet come to a decision. Spencer had said he'd likely be preoccupied—he'd had a meeting with Boyd yesterday.

Upstairs, she knocked on the door to his office. "Mr. Ainsworth?"

The gas lights behind her hissed in the quiet. She glanced over her shoulder at the empty hall. Bringing a hand to the doorknob, she raised her voice. "Mr. Ainsworth, it's Miss Daly."

She opened the door, looked in, and stepped back at once.

Jonathan Ainsworth was quite dead.

He lay on the floor, his desk chair pushed back as though he'd collapsed from it. His face was pallid, his eyes staring in the fixed, unseeing manner of the departed. There was no blood, no gaping wound from which Catherine could discern the cause of his demise. Heart pounding, she crouched down, taking his wrist in some futile attempt to find a pulse. Pieces of a broken teacup were strewn over the floorboards, dark tea splashed across the wood. Ainsworth's skin was already cold, his body stiff, as though he'd been dead for some time, throughout the night even.

Sitting back, she cut her eyes away from his vacant expression. It was startling to stumble upon him like this, but she couldn't find it in herself to shed any tears for her former employer. In place of grief, there was only overwhelming puzzlement, and underlying it, a sharp edge of fear. The sensation coalesced within her heart, and she scrambled to her feet.

She had to tell someone. She had to find Spencer.

In his office downstairs, Spencer sat at his desk, looking over a bit of paper. He jerked his head up when she came in, putting the paper away in a drawer. "Catherine! What—good gracious, can't you knock?"

Catherine closed the door, pressing her back against it. "Spencer," she said. "You need to come upstairs. Mr. Ainsworth— Mr. Ainsworth is dead."

His eyes flew wide. "What? What do you mean?"

"He—I just went up there and, Spencer, it looks like he's been there all night. Did you see him come in this morning?"

Spencer shook his head slowly. "No." He ran a shaking hand through his hair and stood up, coming around the side of the desk. "Oh God, I haven't seen him since yesterday afternoon."

They went up to the fourth floor together. Ainsworth's door hung partially ajar, where Catherine had left it unlatched; through the gap, she saw a chipped fragment of the teacup, part of one of Ainsworth's boots. Spencer eased the door open the rest of the way, and they regarded the body in silence.

After a long moment, Spencer said quietly, "I'll inform the police. I don't know what could've—perhaps the shock of it."

"The shock of what?"

Spencer shuddered, pulling the door closed. Even with Ainsworth's body out of sight, Catherine couldn't rid her mind of the scene. It was as if it were printed on the insides of her eyelids.

Still in that same quiet voice, Spencer said, "He signed over the paper to Mr. Boyd at their meeting yesterday. I thought he might've gone home afterward. I had no idea he was still here." He dragged his fingers through his hair again, his face white as chalk. "I wanted to find you, Catherine, but I wasn't sure where you'd gone. Mr. Boyd may very well let you work here again."

Catherine simply stared at him. The words washed over her, sinking in. Ainsworth had signed away his business. She might return to her work as a printer. She shook her head. "But why would Mr. Ainsworth do such a thing?"

"It's obvious, isn't it?" Spencer's eyes flitted to the closed door. "He was faring poorly. It's why he started the farewell service. It's why he wanted that timepiece." He looked back at her, solemn-faced. "You haven't found it, have you?"

"No." She turned her gaze on the door.

"I'll head to the police station. They'll identify the cause, I'm sure."

"Of course." She reached out then, meaning to place a hand on his arm, but he flinched, and she hid her hands away in her coat pockets. "Spencer," she said. "Are you all right?"

He ignored the question. "I don't know how long I'll be at the station. Will you be here?"

Catherine took a step back down the hall, wanting to put some distance between herself and the door concealing Ainsworth's body. "I need to collect my things," she said hastily. "But I'll come back in the morning."

"Very well."

He made no move to accompany her downstairs, so she left him in the hall, hurrying down the steps. The ground didn't feel quite solid beneath her, and she had to catch hold of the handrail to keep steady.

Spencer had supposed Ainsworth had died of shock. But to her, it looked for all the world like he'd been poisoned.

Stepping out of the building, Catherine blinked in the sunlight. The cold air on her face was a relief for once; it was as if she'd broken free of a nightmare. Only she couldn't cast aside her memories as she might a dream.

"Miss Daly!"

Guy stood waiting on the opposite sidewalk. He took off his hat, waving it at her. A passing carriage pulled to a stop before him, the horses tossing their heads. Guy's face reddened, and he called up apologies to the driver. Then he jammed his hat back on and dashed across the street, bright-eyed and grinning. "Miss Daly," he said. "Thank goodness. I was just about to commence the most magnificent distraction to aid in your escape." He noted her expression, and his eyebrows pinched together. "What's the matter?"

Catherine started away from the print shop. Any minute now, Spencer would be coming through those doors, and she didn't wish for him to find her lingering there.

She told Guy, "Mr. Ainsworth is dead," and the words came out terribly steady. They were the tidy detachment of a death notice set to be printed. Yet as she continued, the steadiness of her voice wavered, drawing thin. "I went up to his office and he—he was on the floor. I think he must've been lying there all night. He was cold."

"My God," said Guy. "Are you quite all right?"

Catherine met his gaze. "It looked like he'd been poisoned, Mr. Nolan. There was a teacup all in pieces on the floor."

A great gust of wind swept past them, and in its wake, she was left trembling, tears pricking at her eyes. "And he signed over the paper to the owner of the *Journal*, so I suppose I may have my job back, but how can I . . . ? How can I go back? Ainsworth was at the university yesterday. He was looking for the timepiece. And now he's dead."

"Miss Daly." Guy's voice was gentle. They came to a stop along the river's edge, and Catherine set a hand upon the parapet wall, the coolness of the damp stone seeping through her glove.

She looked up at Guy's face, at his dark eyes, his kind expression. He asked forthrightly, "What do you want to do?"

She closed her eyes for an instant, taking a breath. "I need to find out what happened to him, Mr. Nolan. If it's connected in any way to the timepiece, we can't let Mr. Smith be caught up in it."

Guy nodded. He looked out over the river. "You're right. Of course you're right." Yet there was a certain strain to his voice, and she could tell something else was weighing on his mind. When he placed his hand on the parapet next to hers, Catherine almost took hold of it.

She said, "I know you're going to the cemetery tonight with Mr. Mallory. Let me come with you."

"Thank you," he said softly. "I'd like that."

They walked on, heading for the watchmaker's shop. Guy stopped at a small bakery, and Catherine welcomed the warmth of it, breathing in the smell of fresh bread, the sweetness of the cakes. They waited their turn at the counter, and she asked, "Is your father at the shop?"

"Yes. And Mr. Smith is upstairs." He turned toward her. "Will you tell Mr. Smith . . . about Mr. Ainsworth?"

"It won't do any good to keep it from him. I believe we've enough trouble already, enough secrets, without adding to the pile."

Guy's mouth quirked. "That's the truth."

He bought a loaf of bread, wrapped it in cloth, and tucked it under his arm. He offered his other arm to Catherine as they stepped back out onto the street. "Sydney will be coming by after dark," he said. "You'll stay for dinner, won't you? I'll tell my father I've invited you and Mr. Smith. It's not often we entertain guests. I think it'll do us all good." He smiled at her, slight but real. "What do you think, Miss Daly?"

"I think that sounds lovely." And she held on to his arm a little tighter.

Dinner at the Nolans' was conducted much the same way as it was back at her family home. Catherine sat beside Owen, across from Guy's father, and she thought again how similar Guy was to Henry, their shared mannerisms. They both gestured with their fork as they talked and leaned back in their chair when they laughed. Catherine missed her parents greatly in that moment, a familiar ache lodging in her heart. She felt a stab of envy, too—how fortunate Guy was he needn't work elsewhere—but that wasn't fair. Guy and Henry were without the rest of their family. Catherine couldn't imagine what it must've been like for Guy's father to lose a wife and two sons in one fell swoop.

Henry retired to bed, and Catherine, Guy, and Owen went down to the shop, into the back room. It was there Catherine told Owen of Ainsworth's demise.

"And you think it has something to do with the timepiece?" Owen asked. He sat next to her on the sofa, his eyes wide as he regarded her.

"It makes the most sense," said Catherine. She looked to Guy, sitting in his chair at the worktable. "But we'll find out for certain."

"If someone poisoned him," Guy started, "that person could be at the print shop."

Catherine swallowed. "I know."

She didn't want to think on it, but it was too glaring to overlook. She wondered about Boyd as well, imagining him sitting in Ainsworth's office, slipping poison into Ainsworth's tea. He'd gotten ownership of his business—perhaps he knew Ainsworth was in search of the timepiece and wanted the device along with the newspaper.

Guy shifted in his chair. Under the lamplight, he arranged things on the desk, straightening the collection of tools. He said, "Mr. Smith, you might want to head upstairs. Sydney will be here momentarily."

Owen stood up. "I can . . . I can come along if you need me to."

"That's all right." Guy smiled. "Miss Daly will be going with us."

Owen's shoulders sagged in obvious relief. He bade them good night, leaving the room just as the clocks chimed in the shop.

Guy began rummaging through one of the desk drawers. He took out an old pocket watch, turned it about in his hand, and nodded to himself, placing it on the tabletop.

"Are you quite set on this, Mr. Nolan?"

"Yes." His eyes shone in the dim light. "I know how it's done. I've seen my father put hours into watches."

"That's not what I meant." Catherine leaned forward. She held his gaze, her hands clasped tight in front of her. "I meant this course of action. Are you quite decided?"

He cast his eyes down to study the floor. "I told you," he said, and his voice shook. "This is what I have to do. At least . . . at least for tonight. I agreed to it." He glanced up at her. "I keep my word, Miss Daly."

"Very well, then. If you insist on being honorable."

A knock sounded at the shop entrance. Guy picked up the watch he'd set aside, a small winding key, and a lantern. Catherine followed him out of the back room, taking her coat from the rack as he pulled open the door.

Sydney Mallory was without a spade, and no cart waited on the street. Catherine supposed they were already at the cemetery. He doffed his hat. "Good evening," he said. "Are you ready?"

"Yes," said Guy.

They headed outside, to where the lamppost in front of the shop glowed, hissing softly, and plumes of factory smoke rose up into the night. Guy closed the door behind him, locking it. And they started off in the direction of the public cemetery.

CHAPTER EIGHTEEN

CATHERINE AND GUY WALKED after Sydney as they made their way through town. Few other pedestrians were about, but a number of carriages clipped by on the road. Light still shone from the windows of terraced houses, the narrow alleyways left in shadow.

To Guy, Catherine said, "We ought to try looking in the old church."

"I agree. Once I . . . When I still time, we can search."

At the cemetery, a horse and cart were stopped at the sidewalk's edge. Two young men sat on the back of the cart, but upon catching sight of them, the pair stood and took up spades and a bundle of canvas cloth before disappearing through the gates.

Sydney came to a standstill at the cart. "You'd best do it now, Guy."

"How much time do you need?"

Head tilted, Sydney considered him. "About two hours. Three would be better."

"For five people . . ." Guy bit at his bottom lip. "That's fifteen hours."

"Can you manage it or not?"

Guy looked away, lighting his lantern, setting it down on the cart. He placed the watch and winding key next to it, then put on his glasses, removed a sewing needle from his coat pocket, and pricked the skin of his palm. "Just give me a moment."

He smeared a bit of blood on the back of the pocket watch. After cleaning his palm with a handkerchief, he fit the winding key into the case to wind the mainspring. He closed his eyes, turning the key, the mechanism clicking softly.

The familiar sounds of the city continued on, but Catherine could imagine, almost sense, the magic drawing around them, pulling close. Three hours, suspended, outside of time. Fifteen hours of Guy's memories.

Silence fell as he pulled the key from the watch. It was a peculiar stillness, an unsettling solitude. The wind ceased, the nearby streetlight no longer flickered. A little ways down the road, a carriage was halted, motionless, horses arrested midstep. Disconcertingly, Guy's watch kept ticking; he stared down at it with a dazed expression.

"I was worried I wouldn't do it right," he murmured.

Sydney asked, "Do we have three hours?" And when Guy nodded, he clapped him on the shoulder. "I'll have your payment to you first thing tomorrow." Lighting another lantern, he lifted a spade from the cart, heading off into the darkness of the cemetery.

Guy took off his spectacles. Lantern light glanced over his features as he tucked the watch and winding key back into his pocket. Turning, he looked up and down the street. "Gracious," he said. "This is strange, isn't it?"

Catherine eyed him. "Are you all right?"

"A little dizzy," he admitted. "I've never done this before."

"Yes, you mentioned so."

He picked up his lantern, using it to gesture toward the gates. "Shall we?"

Yet as they reached them, Guy paused beneath the stone arch. "Miss Daly, wait." His voice was strange, distant. He put the lantern on the ground, and with his other hand, he grabbed hold of the gate. He leaned against it, his temple pressed to the iron bar.

"Mr. Nolan?"

"I don't feel well," he whispered.

A moment later he collapsed, landing in the dirt. The watch slid out of his coat pocket, clacking against the base of the lantern.

Catherine's heart knocked against her rib cage. She knelt beside him, bringing a hand to his shoulder. "Mr. Nolan," she said, frantic. "*Mr. Nolan.*"

He let out a groan and rolled onto his side, his eyes fluttering open. His face was peaky-looking, colorless, but he sat up, his back against the gate. He gazed down at his muddied clothes, his mouth a thin, unhappy line.

"You're not all right," said Catherine.

Fifteen hours of memory. It was little wonder he'd collapsed. Whenever Catherine had made use of magic, she'd given up only an hour at a time.

He swallowed. "I'll be fine."

She helped him to his feet. Putting the watch into her own pocket, she raised Guy's lantern, peering ahead of them. Sydney was nowhere to be seen, but the night was clouded, and shadows lay thick over the grounds.

She wanted to suggest she search alone, to let Guy rest. Before she could, he held out his hand for the lantern. "We mustn't waste this time, Miss Daly. Let's have a look in the church."

They started on the path in that direction. The lantern's light cast a pale glow over the dirt trail, illuminating gnarled tree roots and the etchings on gravestones.

Ainsworth's body was likely spending the night in the hospital morgue. He'd be buried within a vault or under a table tombstone, guarded in Rose Hill from those set on disinterment.

In the near distance, the great heap of the ruins loomed above the graves. It seemed entirely possible that the timepiece could be hidden somewhere inside, away from the prying eyes of resurrection men and cemetery guards.

Guy led the way in, his light a small spot of brightness in the cavernous space. Dry leaves crunched beneath their boots, the smell of damp stone permeating the air. Catherine looked to Guy. "How are you feeling?"

"Well, I've no memory of what I don't remember." He met her gaze, his face unreadable in the dim. "The memories I've lost— I don't know what they were. Though I suppose that's the very nature of losing them."

"I imagine Mr. Smith feels much the same." It was one thing to lose time off her distant future, when she hadn't the knowledge of how long she'd be on this earth. The idea of losing pieces and moments from her past chilled her to the marrow.

Guy's light passed over a stairwell. The stone steps were set in a curve, likely leading to the tower.

Catherine said softly, "Might we try up there?"

The way was narrow and dark as pitch. Guy started up first, saying, "Hold on to my coat," and Catherine did so, placing her other hand on the wall to steady herself. At the top, they found an empty room. There were no parts left from the bells, the windows without slats. The view must've been splendid in the day, but now there was only the river, black and glinting, and the burn of streetlamps between buildings.

Guy raised his lantern, the light catching upon the threads of cobwebs, cracks in the stone, but no timepiece. Catherine took the watch from her pocket, studying the dull silver of the hour and minute hands.

"We can't stay here much longer," she said.

Back downstairs, they stood at the foot of the stairs. Guy held his lantern at his side, peering farther into the hollowed-out church. "I wonder," he said, "if Mr. Smith came back here, whether he might recall something."

Catherine's eyebrows pinched together. "How do you mean?"

"What if he was the one to hide the timepiece, Miss Daly?"

It was a possibility she hadn't considered, one she didn't much care to dwell on. If Owen had hidden the timepiece, he'd surely known of its magic.

"I don't know," she said. "We could . . . we could ask him to come along, I suppose."

Outside the church walls, there came the sound of footsteps. Sydney Mallory appeared in the doorway, a tall silhouette, his spade rested against his shoulder. "We'll be heading off," he told them. "I suggest you do the same. You don't want the watchmen finding you here."

Guy shifted his lantern from one hand to the other. His expression as he regarded Sydney was weary. He said only, "Good night, Sydney."

Sydney took his leave, and the stillness of the night encircled them once more. Catherine reached for the watch in her pocket. The metal was warm to the touch, the ticking faint but audible. When Guy remained silent, she said, "Should we start back?"

"Yes," he murmured.

They walked out of the church, through the cemetery, past the front gates. With lamplight to mark the rest of the way, Guy put out his lantern. There were streaks of mud on his coat and over his boots. Catherine remembered his pocket watch and offered it to him. "Here you are, Mr. Nolan."

He glanced over, his eyes glittering in the dim. It took her a moment to realize he was crying. "Mr. Nolan," she said, "whatever is the matter?"

Guy took the watch in his hand, letting out a hitched breath. "What I did tonight was neither good nor honorable. I've used magic when my father told me I oughtn't. I've lied to him. I thought . . . I thought I could put things right. I thought this was the way." He scrubbed at his eyes, his voice wavering as he continued. "Is this what my mother would have me do? My brothers? I think not."

"Mr. Nolan." Catherine put a gloved hand over his, the one holding the watch. "You're doing your best. That's all we can ever do."

He pulled away. Closing his eyes, he ducked his head, tears slipping down his face. "I don't know what to do, Miss Daly." He sniffed. "I—I don't—"

They both startled as the city's stillness shattered around them. It was far from the bustle of midday, but the preceding silence made everything seem louder than it was. The wind gusted, the streetlamp hissed, carriage wheels squeaked and bumped over the cobbles. Time went on, and so did the people, carried by the tide of it.

Guy wiped at his face with his coat sleeve. "I need to get home," he said, his voice a little hoarse. "Will you—are you coming along, Miss Daly?"

She nodded. She didn't trust herself to speak in that moment. They walked toward the watchmaker's, passing other rows of shops. Cheery light emanated from some of the flats above, but at this hour, most of the windows were dark, lace curtains drawn across them for the night. Awnings were pulled down, CLOSED signs upon the doors.

Quietly, Guy said, "Are you going back to the *Chronicle* tomorrow?"

"Yes. I'm to meet Mr. Boyd, the new proprietor." Catherine fidgeted with the ties of her bonnet. "Might I have some paper when we get in? I'd like to write to my family."

"Certainly." After a pause, he added, even quieter, "I'd like to hear more about them, if you're inclined to tell me."

And so she did. She spoke of her mother and father, how good and kind they were. She recalled times when she and John and Anne had rolled down wet hills in the rain, when they'd fallen asleep in the fields on summer nights. A lump rose in the back of her throat, her vision blurring as they neared the green front of the watchmaker's shop. At the front step, Guy looked to her, and his eyes widened. "Apologies," he said. "I've upset you."

Catherine smiled even as she wiped the tears from her cheeks. "No, no. You're quite all right, Mr. Nolan."

He turned away. Bringing a hand to the door, he picked at a flake of peeling green paint. He said something, but she didn't catch what it was.

"Pardon?"

"I said you may call me Guy, if you like." In the lamplight, she saw the flush of pink across his face. "We're friends, aren't we?"

"In that case," she said, voice soft, "you must call me Catherine."

Guy smiled at her, his eyes bright. He said, "Catherine," as if only for the sake of it, the delight of doing so.

She grinned back. "Yes, Guy?"

He ducked his head, blushing still, and took out his key. "I'll fetch you some paper," he said, opening the door.

They sat together in the kitchen as she wrote her letter.

Tending to the fire, Guy said, "I plan on going to the chemist's tomorrow."

Catherine paused in her writing. A lit candle before her on the table cast warm light over the still wet ink. She said, "There's medicines that might be used as poisons. If we made inquiries—if anyone from the print shop bought something of such a nature, that would help greatly in narrowing down suspects."

"We need to determine what sort of poison was used," said Guy. He set down the poker, leaning an arm against the mantelpiece. "There's plenty of things that can work as a poison. If indeed Mr. Ainsworth was poisoned. Are you quite certain?"

Catherine put aside her pen. "I think his body will be in the hospital morgue."

Understanding flashed in Guy's eyes. "Miss Daly," he said. "Catherine, I'm not sure anyone there would tell us anything."

"How else are we to get answers?"

From down the hall, a door cracked open. Footsteps sounded on the floorboards, and Owen appeared in the kitchen doorway. "You might've told me you were in."

Guy stepped away from the mantel. There were shadows beneath his eyes, accentuated by the firelight. "You were asleep, Mr. Smith."

"Is everything all right?" Owen asked. "Did you go to the cemetery?"

"Yes." Guy dragged a hand through his hair. "We didn't manage to find the timepiece, unfortunately."

"We were just discussing Mr. Ainsworth," said Catherine. Her gaze returned to her letter, the sweep of her cursive across the page. "I'll head to the print shop in the morning and see what I can find out."

Owen said, "Good night, then." He rubbed at his eyes and curled his other hand around the doorframe. "You both ought to get some sleep."

He went back down the hall, the bedroom door closing, and Guy came over to the table. His voice was almost a whisper as he said, "Are you still writing your letter?"

"I'm almost finished." Catherine looked up at him. "Guy— what will you do?"

He seemed to know what she meant. He let out a sigh and lowered his gaze, his fingers tracing the dark knots in the table. "I'll figure something out. Perhaps we can open the shop for longer hours."

"You should rest," she told him. "I'll head downstairs in a moment."

He looked at her. "I'm not all that tired," he said, and smiled.

He returned to the fireplace, nudged the logs with his poker, then picked up a slim brown book from the small pile of volumes on the mantelpiece. He dropped into the flowered armchair, and for a moment, Catherine looked over his tousled hair, the curve of his shoulder, watching as he slid his reading glasses onto his nose. She went back to her letter, and sitting there in Guy's company, she felt a quiet calm, easing her heart a little of her worries.

Once she finished writing, she sealed the letter in an envelope. She rose from her chair, took hold of the candle, and Guy set down his book, glancing up at her. He stood and clasped his hands behind his back. "Thank you again for coming along tonight," he said.

Catherine tilted her head to the side. "I ought to be thanking you. We're going back there, aren't we? We didn't search all of the church."

"Indeed. There was quite a bit of debris about the place from what I could tell. It looked ghostly."

The shop clocks began to chime the hour. The sound of the tolling eerily underlined Guy's words, and they both smiled, laughing softly. Catherine's candlelight reflected in his spectacles, a small, wavering glow. She cleared her throat as the last of the chimes fell silent, her voice coming out as a whisper. "Good night, Guy."

Still smiling, he said, "Good night."

Catherine left the kitchen, holding her candle aloft, and made her way downstairs.

CHAPTER NINETEEN

CATHERINE READIED HERSELF for the day in near darkness. She lit the lamp in the back room and dressed in a flurry, pulling on her stockings and boots, tying her corset and petticoats over her chemise, slipping into her dress. She met Guy and Owen for breakfast with her face scrubbed clean and her hair pinned tightly.

"Will you be heading to the park, Mr. Smith?" she asked.

He shook his head, fidgeting with his teacup. "I think I'll ask around about an apprenticeship."

Meeting Catherine's gaze, Guy said, "I'll come by the print shop later. We can go to the chemist's together."

Catherine nodded. She ate a few bites of toast and drank some tea, even as her stomach knotted in apprehension. It was possible Boyd wouldn't give her a job. It was possible he had poisoned Ainsworth.

She and Owen bundled into their coats and hats, setting off

down the street. After some minutes, Owen said, "You don't look too keen on this, Miss Daly."

Catherine gave a little, choked laugh, the sound catching in her throat. "I suppose I'm not. Mr. Boyd may very well be a killer."

"Or," said Owen, "he may be a perfectly kind and considerate employer."

"Well, yes, I'd much prefer that."

They reached the *Invercarn Chronicle*, and it was as though Catherine was seeing it anew. She hadn't truly realized how dark the brickwork was, the grime that blotted the edges of the windowpanes, the soot-covered chimney tops. She could see the place that was once Ainsworth's office, up on the fourth floor. The curtains were pulled across the window. Everything appeared still.

"Take care, please, Miss Daly," Owen said.

Before all this had started, Bridget had spoken similar words. *Be careful, won't you, Catherine?*

"I will," she told Owen now. "You take care too."

Inside the shop, the print floor looked the same as ever. It was too early for anyone to be at work, and the presses shone clean, the desks tidied, the row of type cabinets neat and orderly beside one another. She took to the stairs, heading up to the third floor. Easing open the door to her former room, she found Bridget fast asleep. She lit a candle and said, "Bridget. Bridget, wake up."

Bridget's eyes blinked open, squinting in the candlelight. "Catherine." She sat up against the headboard, wide-awake in an instant. "Spencer told me what happened. Are you all right? Have you come back? Mr. Boyd will surely let you work here again."

"That's what I'm hoping." Catherine sat at the desk chair. "What about the farewell service? He's not continuing with that, is he?"

"No. No, that's quite in the past, he said. It's only print work."

Catherine's gaze flicked to the candle atop the desk. The flame twisted and sputtered, stirred by her breath. "Has he said anything of Mr. Ainsworth's death? The cause of it?"

When Bridget didn't answer, Catherine looked back at her. She was wringing her hands, brow furrowed. Strands of her pale hair had loosened from her plait in the night, curling about her face. Finally, she said, "Mr. Boyd hasn't spoken much of it. I don't suppose he cares to dwell on such dreadfulness. But Spencer told me the police believe he died of apoplexy."

Catherine frowned. "What does that mean?"

"Sudden death," whispered Bridget. "They say he was bleeding on the inside."

Could poison do such a thing? Catherine felt at once entirely out of her depth.

"I heard he had you searching for that timepiece," Bridget said, still in quiet tones. "It wasn't right, what he did."

Rubbing at her temple, Catherine murmured, "I never did find it. The timepiece."

"No one will, Catherine. It's only a tale."

Catherine got up, smoothing out her skirts without meeting Bridget's eye. The timepiece was far from a tale—that much she knew. It was magic that had brought Owen back to life. "I'm going to wait for Mr. Boyd downstairs. I'm sorry for waking you."

Bridget reached out, clasping one of Catherine's hands in hers. "Don't apologize for that. I was worried—I hadn't any idea where you went." She tilted her head. "Where *did* you go?"

Catherine hesitated, then wondered why she did. There was no harm in telling Bridget of her time spent at the watchmaker's shop. She'd already told Spencer about asking for Guy's help. And yet something had changed. Now the way before her felt perilous; things she didn't think to be secrets became so.

Owen's voice echoed in her mind. *Take care.*

"Here and there," Catherine replied lightly. "I'll let you know what Mr. Boyd says."

Back downstairs, she wandered along the lines of presses. She remembered learning how to set type, how to lock it into a chase with furniture and quoins. It was fine work, a good wage.

She went to her desk, but it was clear of notes. There was nothing to mark her presence, not here nor in her room. Her belongings were still packed away in her trunk in the Nolans' flat.

The shop door opened, the bell above it chiming.

"Hello there." The voice was mild, pleasant, and Catherine turned to find Boyd at the front entrance. He doffed his hat, removed his overcoat, hanging both on the rack.

"Good morning, Mr. Boyd." Catherine folded her hands in front of her. "I've been wanting to speak with you. I'm Miss Catherine Daly."

"Miss Daly, yes." Boyd smiled. "Mr. Carlyle made mention of you." He started toward the desks, gesturing for her to follow. "I was rather hoping you'd return. Most intriguing, your story."

Interestingly, he didn't lead her upstairs to what was previously Ainsworth's office. Instead, he went to the back office on the print floor, a place Catherine regarded as Spencer's during the workday. Boyd answered her confusion, saying, "I'm afraid neither myself nor Mr. Carlyle wish to make use of the upstairs office for the time being. This is not how I imagined beginning my proprietorship, but lo! Here we are. Good gracious. Take a seat, please, Miss Daly." He settled behind the desk, and Catherine sat in the chair in front of it.

"Mr. Boyd, I'm not sure what Mr. Carlyle has told you about—about my dismissal."

"Oh, the whole of it, I believe." He leaned back in his chair, his smile knowing. "I'm quite aware of the fact you don't have the timepiece Mr. Ainsworth was after. I certainly doubt you would be here if you did."

"I don't, sir." Catherine held his gaze, bracing herself. "I only want to return to my work as a compositor. I did a fair job in Mr. Ainsworth's employ."

"Yes, Mr. Carlyle has assured me of your proficiency. You're most welcome back to your position, Miss Daly. I've enough to manage at the moment without looking for another to take your place."

They were the words she'd hoped to hear, but they didn't ease her disquiet. Had Boyd been in Ainsworth's office when he died? Had he smiled just as he smiled at her now?

Catherine inclined her head. "Thank you, sir," she said, grateful when her voice remained steady. "I'm much obliged."

"I should be thanking you, Miss Daly. I'm glad you wish to come back after what occurred." He eyed a pile of papers set to one side of the desk before returning his attention to her. "I won't be carrying on the farewell service this establishment offered under Mr. Ainsworth's management. I assume that's agreeable to you?"

She nodded.

Boyd went on. "I don't mean to speak ill of the dead, but the way he conducted business was entirely wrong. I very much want to do better by all of you employed here."

Catherine did not know if he truly meant it. All the same, she replied, "That's gracious of you, sir."

Outside the office door, there was movement—the scrape of chairs, the shuffling of paper. Boyd stood up to show her out. "I'll give you the day to get things in order," he said. "But I'll expect you at work tomorrow morning."

"Yes. Thank you again, Mr. Boyd."

She hurried upstairs to tell Bridget the news. And after Bridget went down to the print shop, Catherine stayed in their room for a time. She sat at the desk, looking over the loose bits of paper, the collection of inkpots—most of them nearly empty—and the tidy arrangement of pens. She reached across and cracked open the window, letting in some fresh air, watching the sway of the lace curtains in the breeze. The open window also let in the noise of the waking city. People called to one another on the street, and coach wheels clattered over the cobbles.

Catherine leaned forward, gazing at the sleek black tops of passing carriages, gentlemen crossing the road dressed in fine cloaks and silk hats. She caught sight of a familiar young man as he came into view, walking down the opposite sidewalk. He held a newspaper in his gloved hands, his head bent as he read. He seemed so absorbed by whatever was on the page, he passed right by the print shop. A laugh escaped her as, a few minutes later, he reappeared, having doubled back.

Guy Nolan stopped in front of the *Chronicle*. He peered up at the windows, and Catherine pulled her own window shut, grinning as she made her way down to meet him.

He crossed the street in all swiftness when he saw her.

"Did you speak with Mr. Boyd?"

"Yes. He's expecting me back tomorrow to start work."

Guy smiled, but the next instant, his expression turned worried. "That's good," he said. "I mean, isn't it? If he's not a murderer, that is."

"If he's not a murderer," Catherine echoed. She nodded to the paper he carried. "Why've you brought that?"

His smile returned, his eyes lighting up behind his spectacles. "I wanted to show you." He flipped the newspaper to the advertisements. "I purchased it a couple of weeks ago, before"— he made a sweeping gesture with one hand—"all this happened."

Catherine studied the page.

In a small section was an advertisement for the watchmaker's shop:

> *H. Nolan & Son*
> *WATCH REPAIR*
> *Exact and ready attention will be paid to all kinds*
> *of Watches and Clocks. Shop at 20 Oak Street.*

Guy said, "Isn't it fine? What brilliant timing. This is just what we need."

Catherine looked up at him. "It's lovely. Well printed and concise."

"Yes, I thought so." Guy's cheeks flushed pink. He tucked the newspaper into his coat, offering her his arm as they started away from the print shop. "So, pray tell, what did you find out? Does anyone know the cause of Mr. Ainsworth's death?"

"Apparently he was bleeding on the inside."

Guy gave a shudder. "That sounds unpleasant," he remarked.

"Perhaps there's some poison capable of doing that. I really do think we ought to go to the morgue, Guy."

"We can go there," he said, "but I'm not certain we'll get any answers."

They first paid a visit to the chemist's shop.

Guy doffed his hat, opening the door. Inside, wall-to-wall shelves were laden with glass jars and bottles. An elderly lady was making a purchase at the counter. While they waited, Catherine asked, "What do you need in here?"

"My father's medicine. It helps him sleep."

Catherine looked about at the medicines: small, neat labels on the vials, bottles with cork stoppers, cloth-covered jars. They crowded the countertop as well as the shelves, glass catching the light of the lamps. Dust drifted in the air, but the counter was quite clear of it, the dark wood polished. The man standing behind it was gray-haired, his forehead lined with deep wrinkles. As the lady left the shop, the man glanced to Guy. He turned back to the shelves, fetching a vial and setting it on the counter without Guy needing to ask for it. The glass clicked against the varnished wood.

"Thank you, Mr. Brooke," said Guy, taking coins from his pocket.

"Sir," Catherine started, "this may seem an odd question, but could any medicines here bring about apoplexy?"

Brooke's eyebrows rose. "Indeed, an odd question. Why are you concerned about such a thing?"

"Apologies, sir." Catherine shook her head. "I was only curious."

She and Guy left the shop, stepping back outside, and Guy patted the pocket that held his father's medicine. He said, "This whole thing gives me the shivers. Mr. Smith's murderer could still be alive and well, for all we know. It could even be the same person."

"It's possible."

Guy was quiet for a moment. "I can't help but wonder," he said, "if more dreadfulness is yet to happen, if we've only just stepped into the dark." He brought a hand to his heart. "It's like a shadow hanging over me, and I don't much care for it."

• • •

The city hospital was a two-story building of gray stone and brick near the university. The front gates opened into a courtyard, and a few carriages were stationed outside the carriage house. Catherine gazed up at the sash windows as they headed for the entrance. Once they were inside, the double doors swung shut behind them with an ominous thud.

"Which way to the morgue, do you think?" asked Guy.

There was no sign of where it might be located. Catherine started down a dimly lit hall, noting the rooms that lay beyond the doors. In most, there were rows of simple iron beds, doctors tending to patients. They ended up circling back, trying another hallway, before they happened upon the marked room for the mortuary.

Guy tried the door. It was locked.

He said, "Do you suppose we should just wait until someone comes along?"

Catherine peered through the glass set into the door. Whereas other rooms in the hospital held neatly made beds, the morgue contained only a row of metal tables, the bodies atop them covered in white sheets. The lamps burned brightly in their wall brackets, illuminating instruments on the counters, a washstand and basin.

"Catherine," Guy whispered urgently. Then, sounding overly cheerful, he said, "Good day, sir."

Catherine turned around in a hurry. A young man made his way toward them, his expression guarded. He looked to be about twenty or so, perhaps one of the attendants. He said, "Good day. Can I help you with something?"

"Yes," said Catherine. "My late employer, Jonathan Ainsworth—is he here?"

"Ainsworth?" There was a flash of something in his expression, a spark to his gaze. "No, I'm afraid not, miss. The examiner already signed off on his report."

"What was the cause of his death? Do you know it?"

The attendant came over to where they stood. "We detected arsenic in his stomach," he said after a pause. He glanced past Catherine to the mortuary door. "It can be mistaken for apoplexy, or cholera. The quantity would've killed him quickly, similar to apoplexy."

Catherine felt her insides twist. "Arsenic?"

"Do the police know?" Guy asked.

"They have the report, yes."

Catherine's heart hammered. She saw again the shattered tea-cup on the floor, the blank stare of Ainsworth's gaze.

Neither she nor Guy spoke until they were back outside the hospital. Standing in the courtyard, Guy said, "It's not the way Mr. Smith was murdered, if his dream was indeed a memory."

"I don't think it's the same killer." Catherine turned to him, dread working through her veins. "It's likely someone at the print shop poisoned Mr. Ainsworth."

A sharp gust of wind lifted the fallen leaves off the ground. They tumbled over the cobbles, fetching up against the carriage house. Catherine pulled her coat close. "When I return tomor-row," she said, "I'm going to search."

"For arsenic? Catherine, you can't be caught poking around. If whoever did this knows you suspect something, I can't imagine they'll be pleased."

She started for the front gates. Just down the street, there were the university buildings, weather-darkened and imposing, their clay chimney pots set against the overcast sky.

Guy fell into step beside her. "Where are we going?"

"I'd like to pay a call on Mr. Williams," she said. "I saw Mr.

Boyd at the university the other day. I want to know what he was doing there."

"You suppose he's after the timepiece as well?"

"When I spoke to him, he said he knew I didn't have it." Catherine ducked her head against the wind. "He may have said that because he knows it's still out there. Perhaps he discovered where it might be from someone at the university."

"Mr. Williams didn't seem very knowledgeable on the subject," Guy put in.

They reached the same building Sydney had brought them to. Up on the fourth floor, Catherine knocked on Francis's door, and this time, he answered.

"Well, hello," he said. "Miss Daly, yes? And Mr. Nolan?"

Catherine smiled. "Good morning, Mr. Williams."

He was dressed tidily—his shirt collar starched, his trousers pressed—but he also looked like he'd been up half the night and then some. "What can I do for you? Is Mr. Mallory here?"

"No, it's only us," said Catherine. "May we come in?"

Francis scratched the back of his neck, his expression more than a little puzzled. "Of course," he said, his tone well mannered despite his bewilderment. "Would you like tea?"

Guy had been gazing down the hall, but now he looked over and said, "Yes, thank you."

They settled in chairs around the fireplace, the flames flickering in the grate. Catherine felt cold nonetheless; she hadn't taken off her coat. Fear had burrowed into her heart like a splinter. "Mr. Williams," she said, "last time we were here, I noticed Mr. Boyd from the *Journal*. Are you acquainted with him?"

"Oh, yes, Mr. Boyd. He's a fine fellow, I think."

Catherine clutched her teacup. "Do you know what he was doing here? Was he asking about the timepiece?"

Francis tipped his head to the side, regarding her. "Still looking for it, are you?"

"Mr. Ainsworth, my former employer, wished to find it. Now he's dead. Someone poisoned him."

His eyes widened a little. "Poisoned? How so?"

"We've just come from the hospital. An attendant there told us it was arsenic." Catherine didn't look away from him. "Was Mr. Boyd inquiring about the timepiece or not, Mr. Williams?"

"I don't believe so," he replied. "But he was—about a fortnight ago. There was word going around it was buried in an unmarked plot."

Catherine sat back in her chair. When she closed her eyes, she saw Owen as he looked in the cemetery, pale-faced, standing at the edge of his grave.

"What about Mr. Ainsworth? You said he was here the other day."

Francis frowned. "Mr. Ainsworth? I haven't seen him in some time."

Catherine lowered her teacup, narrowing her eyes. "You mentioned a man from the *Chronicle* was asking around about the timepiece."

"Oh, but not Mr. Ainsworth." Francis's gaze shifted to the fire as he took up the poker. Shadows flitted across his face. "I can't recall his name now. I thought he was a student."

Catherine shared a look with Guy. His eyes met hers, dark and wondering, but Catherine could venture a guess as to who Francis meant. "Mr. Carlyle?" she said.

"Ah, yes." Francis smiled, placing the poker back against the wall. "That might've been it. As I said, I didn't speak to him myself."

Catherine pressed her lips thin, staring into her tea. Spencer could've been on an errand for Ainsworth, but if so, she wondered why he hadn't told her of it.

In the chair next to her, Guy said, "Thank you, Mr. Williams." Turning toward Catherine, his voice quieted, rising softly in a question. "Shall we be on our way?"

But when they got outside, they were met with rain falling in sheets. The two of them waited beneath the entranceway, watching it pour down across the curve of stone above their heads. The courtyard was already miry, marked with puddles, the sight to the road a blur of gray, rain striking the wrought-iron fence in the distance.

"It'll let up in a moment," Guy said. He held his hat at his side, and his hair was tangled, made wavy by the damp air. He pushed a lock of it out of his eyes, looking over at her. "Are you all right?"

Catherine put her hands in her coat pockets. "I don't know why Spencer would be asking about the timepiece. Unless he was asking on Mr. Ainsworth's behalf." She gazed out at the rain, and the steadiness of it, however battering, calmed her nerves. This was the way it rained back home, too—consistent and relentless in the colder months.

Guy said, "Are we going to the cemetery tonight? We've yet to ask Mr. Smith."

"And what are we to do if he does remember? If he did hide the timepiece?"

"Then we'll know," Guy said simply. "And if he did not, it's possible he might remember who did." He surveyed the way ahead of them, his expression creasing in concern. "I do hope he's not caught in this rain."

They fell silent, waiting, both of them looking out from the shadows of the arch. Guy stood near to her, near enough

Catherine felt the brush of his arm against hers. The sound of carriages on the street was muffled by the pounding rain, and the world seemed small, close, just she and Guy in the slate-gray November morning.

CHAPTER TWENTY

IT WAS MIDAFTERNOON by the time Catherine and Guy made
it through the rain to the watchmaker's shop. In the back room,
Guy sat at the worktable, carefully piecing a pocket watch together
after having cleaned it. Catherine sat on the sofa behind him,
wishing she could piece together what she'd learned at the morgue
with what she was still missing as easily as Guy could reassemble
watches.

Henry Nolan was upstairs in the flat, but at times he came down
to the shop. He polished the clocks or looked in on them, considering
Guy's work. Catherine understood little of the conversation when
the two discussed watch repair, but she liked listening all the same.
It was always pleasing, she thought, to see someone doing what they
did best, how it steadied them, the light in their eyes. She knew Guy
enjoyed his trade, enjoyed it as she did hers. It was evident in the

carefulness of his hands, the earnestness in his voice.

Henry didn't seem to mind her being there, either. He brought her tea, smiled at her, and Catherine was reminded of her own father making her tea in the mornings.

Owen had yet to return. When Catherine noted his absence, Guy said, "He's likely going about shops all over the city. Someone will take him on eventually, I'm sure."

"Certainly so," replied Catherine.

Guy adjusted the magnifying loupe he wore over his spectacles. The watch was secured in a movement holder beneath the glow of his lamp, light shining through its emerald glass shade. "I wonder if he might be interested in watchmaking." He glanced back at her. "Or do you think he might like print work?"

"I suppose if he's not printing obituaries. It's too morbid for his liking. He doesn't wish to work as a coffin maker again." Without meaning to, Catherine thought of the dream Owen had described to them, and a shiver crept up her spine. "Why would someone murder him, Guy?"

Guy paused in his work. "I've wondered the same," he said, voice low. "But it was years ago. We might never know."

Catherine couldn't bear it, the not knowing. She leaned forward on the sofa. "Do you think his murder has something to do with the timepiece?"

Putting aside his tweezers, Guy rubbed the back of his neck. "I don't see how it could be—unless the timepiece belonged to him. He could've been murdered for plenty of other reasons. I'm not sure how we'll solve it when we've so little information to go on." He ran his fingers along the desk's edge. The dark wood was scratched in numerous places, marks from watchmaking tools and years of use. "I do think it strange that the timepiece didn't bring him back any sooner. Why now?"

Catherine swallowed. "And why hasn't it worked on anyone else?"

Guy took off his spectacles, turning around to face her. The lamp behind him hissed softly, the clocks in the next room all ticking at once. Catherine wanted quite badly to ask what Henry Nolan's nightmares were about, why he'd allowed himself to lose so many memories selling time to people. Instead, she said, "If the timepiece is in that cemetery, it must be in the church. It would've likely been picked up by now if it were elsewhere on the grounds."

"Perhaps Mr. Williams is right." Guy fidgeted with his glasses. "Perhaps it's tucked away in a shop someplace."

From outside the back room, the bell above the front door chimed. And then there was Owen's voice, saying, "Mr. Nolan? Hello?" He reached the doorway, looking in at them, and evidently he'd been out in the rain. The shoulder cape of his overcoat was damp, the hat in his hands dripping water onto the floor. He winced. "Sorry. I'll clean that up. Hello, Miss Daly. How did things go at the print shop?"

Guy looked despairingly at the puddle as Owen shrugged off his coat and took a seat beside Catherine on the sofa. She said, "Well, I have my job back. And we visited the morgue. Mr. Ainsworth was poisoned with arsenic."

"My word, have you two just been sitting here discussing murder?"

Guy grimaced and began tidying his work space. Catherine said, "You seem in a pleasant mood, Mr. Smith. Did you secure an apprenticeship?"

With a sigh, Owen fell back against the cushions. The color was high in his cheeks from the chill air, his hazel eyes dark. "Unfortunately, no one had need of me." He turned his head to look at her. "What am I to do, Miss Daly? I need direction."

"You can accompany us to the cemetery, if you like. We're going to have another look in the church ruins."

Owen blanched. He looked Guy's way and stood up, leaning his hands upon the worktable. He gazed over the strewn instruments and pocket watches. "You're set on this venture as well, Mr. Nolan?"

Guy took the magnifying loupe from his glasses and put it aside. The watch remained suspended in the movement holder, golden gears exposed. "We were rather hoping you'd come with us, Mr. Smith. All the better to have you along—and you might remember something."

"Watchmen patrol the cemetery, don't they?" said Owen.

"Sometimes," Guy said, and then added, "We'll be careful."

Owen frowned. "I've already been murdered once, thank you very much. I'm not keen on giving someone else a chance."

Standing up, Catherine placed a hand on his arm. "We won't be there all night. Mr. Nolan and I already had a look around. We need only search the rest of the church."

When the three of them reached the cemetery gates, the sun had set. Clouds and coal dust obscured the starlight, and the shadows stretched long across the dirt pathways. The old church looked to be another sepulcher in the darkness, a mass of weathered stone between the trees.

The lantern Guy held was their only light source. Catherine walked beside him, the flame within the glass illuminating the muddy earth and rain-slicked grave markers. They moved off the trail, heading over the wet grass. Owen slipped, and Guy caught him by the arm, hauling him upright.

"I did not think I'd be back here so soon," said Owen. "After—after that night, I did not want to set foot here again."

"Well, eventually, we all head back here, don't we?" Catherine said.

"My, that's grim. Though," Guy added, raising the lantern, "we ought to take care. I've heard one of those stones fall, and the sound alone almost sent me to my grave."

Catherine saw what Guy meant as they approached the church. Large blocks of stone were scattered about the grass, some of them grown over with moss and lichen. The church was missing a piece of exterior wall, the roof partly caved in. Perhaps in time it would wear away to nothing.

As they neared, Catherine caught movement at the entrance. She held out an arm, bringing Guy and Owen to a stop. "Wait," she said.

A person stood at the doorway, a man indistinguishable aside from his dark coat and hat. He started back toward the main gates, head ducked, walking across the grounds with the same confident familiarity as she did.

It was her foreman, Spencer Carlyle.

She almost called out to him—yet the surrounding quiet and the briskness of his pace brought her up short. In a whisper, she said, "It's Spencer Carlyle. I don't know what he's doing here." She looked around to Guy and Owen, the two of them standing wide-eyed and still. Guy's lantern light flickered over their faces, turning them ghostly.

"He was asking about the timepiece," Guy said, his voice hushed. "He's likely looking for it, just as we are."

Once Spencer was out of sight, they made their way toward the gloomy heap of stone. At the doorway, Catherine peered inside.

Timber beams arched across the ceiling, the floor space cleared of pews. Dead leaves and branches collected at the base of the rough stone walls, carried in by the wind. She took a step over the threshold, Guy following with the lantern. There was no evidence of what Spencer could've been doing in here. Guy's light made strange patterns against the walls, flashing upon the twisted branches on the floor, the uneven stone. Owen came after them, and Catherine turned to see him holding on to the brim of his hat, his head tilted back as he peered into the broken rafters.

His voice cracked as he said, "What if there's something up there?"

Catherine shuddered. The words painted a visceral picture in her mind of someone watching from above, clinging to the rotten beams like a nightmarish gargoyle.

"Yes," replied Guy. "Dust and cobwebs. That's all."

Catherine headed through the empty nave to where the roof had collapsed, the jagged hole revealing the night sky. A gust of wind blew in, the splintered beams groaning.

"Catherine," Guy said, his tone threaded with anxiety. "Be careful."

"Bring the light," she told him. "I can hardly see."

Guy and Owen walked over the detritus toward her. The lantern light shone across a section of wall that enclosed a small room, as dark and empty as the rest of the church. Catherine ducked under the lintel, her stomach giving a sickening lurch as she missed a step at the threshold. "Mind," she told the boys, "there's a step here."

Hatless, Guy's head almost brushed the ceiling. Owen stepped in after him and asked, "What is this? A cellar?"

"Coal cellar, possibly," said Guy.

The room was chilly and smelled faintly of rot, the stones holding in the damp. Catherine studied the ground, hoping to catch the shine of glass, a metal casing. Instead, Guy's lantern flashed upon soot marks on the wall, bits of coal left in the corners. A hatch door was set into the floor. There was a ring pull handle, heavy and rusted. Catherine crouched down, bringing her hand to it, feeling the chill of the metal through her glove. She gave the handle a tug, but the door wouldn't shift.

"Here," said Guy, putting his lantern down. "We shall try it together."

He took hold of the ringed handle alongside her. She glanced at his face—so close to hers, his cheeks flushed from the cold—before fixing her attention on the door. They pulled hard, and the door swung free, so suddenly Guy lost his balance, tumbling against the stone wall behind them. He sat up and rubbed the back of his head.

"Are you all right?" Catherine asked.

"Fine," he said with a grimace.

She looked away from him, peering down at the hole in the floor. The light of the lantern didn't offer much illumination; there was a ladder at the opening, and below it, darkness.

"I hope you don't expect me to climb down there," said Owen.

Guy stood up, dusting off his hands. "I'll go," he said. "It's likely another part of the cellar, a storeroom."

Catherine reached down and pushed at the ladder, testing it. It held firm, but she said, "I don't know, Guy. How far down does this ladder go? What if it breaks?"

"Then you'll have to rescue me." He smiled brightly.

Owen said, "Oh, goodness."

After Guy took the first couple of rungs of the ladder, Catherine passed him the lantern, the light withdrawing from the room as he went farther down. She shivered, knowing that if he dropped it, they might be left in the dark.

A sharp, splintering *crack* sent her heart hammering. Guy let out a short cry, the light swinging wildly down below. Catherine's hands gripped the edge of the opening.

"Guy!"

"I'm all right," he called. "The last rung just broke. I'm at the bottom now."

"What's down there?" asked Owen.

"Not much of anything." Guy coughed. "Lots of dust. There's some old crates." He moved away from the ladder, his voice growing muffled. There came a rasp of wood, a thud, as though he was searching the boxes.

Yet there was another sound—quiet but unmistakable—from beyond the church walls. Footfalls, boots squelching through mud. Catherine stood, her gaze flitting to the doorway, to the darkness of the field past the missing piece of wall. A light flashed between the graves, and her blood went cold.

"Miss Daly?" said Owen.

She turned back to him. "Get down there," she told him, pointing to the ladder. "There's a watchman just outside."

His eyes widened. Wringing his hands, he started, "Miss Daly, I—"

"Hurry." Fear tore at her insides, panic closing around her heart.

He hunched his shoulders, mouth pressed thin, but he reached for the ladder to make his way down.

Below them, Guy's voice: "Is something wrong?"

Catherine didn't answer him but went down the ladder after Owen. She saw the glow of Guy's lantern at the bottom, heard him say, "Here, Mr. Smith," offering his hand as he helped Owen, then her, past the cracked rung.

"A watchman is out there," Catherine whispered. Guy peered up the length of the ladder, but she grabbed him by the sleeve. "Mind your light."

They moved farther into the storeroom, Guy leading them to the empty crates piled in a corner. He turned one over and sat on it, setting his lantern on the dirt floor.

There was a small cut on his face, just above his jaw. The line of blood shone bright red in the light. Catherine said, "You're bleeding."

Guy gave her a blank look. "Pardon?"

She touched the place on her own face, and Guy put a hand to his cheek. He studied the blood on his fingertips, brow furrowed. "I must've got it when the rung gave way." Glancing to her, he asked, "Is it very bad?"

"It's just a scratch." She took out her handkerchief, passing it to him.

He brought the cloth to his face and leaned back, glancing around. "This is cozy. How long are we to stay down here?"

The ceiling at this part of the storeroom was quite low; Owen raised a hand, his palm resting flat against it. "It feels like I'm back there." His voice was unsteady. "In the grave."

Guy made a sympathetic sound. "Oh, Mr. Smith." He turned over two other crates and said, "Here now, come sit."

"We just have to wait for the guard to move on," said Catherine, taking a seat. "And we must be quiet."

They sat in silence for some minutes, before Guy murmured, "The timepiece . . . It doesn't look to be here, either."

The room was bare aside from the crates, the packed-dirt floor clear of debris. Through the cellar opening, Catherine could make out the whistling of the wind. She put her arms about herself. "Mr. Smith, do you recall anything? Being back here?"

He ducked his head, rubbing his palms together. "No, Miss Daly."

Getting up, she began to search through the remainder of the crates. Guy stood as well, lantern in hand, giving her more light. The boxes were splitting along the grain, damp-stained—all of them empty. With a sigh, she shook her head.

Guy took a step back. "I'll go and see if the guard has gone." He headed up the ladder, and Catherine and Owen waited in the dark.

Minutes slipped past. Catherine closed her eyes against the dim, her nerves fraying as time went on. Owen fidgeted and asked, "Do you suppose he's all right?"

Then—

"Miss Daly? Mr. Smith?"

Catherine scrambled to her feet. She curled both hands around a ladder rung, letting out a breath of relief upon finding Guy at the opening. "We were wondering where you got to."

She saw the flash of his grin. "Come up," he said. "I don't see anyone about. I think we're quite safe now."

Catherine gestured for Owen to go up first. Once she reached the top herself, Guy carefully pulled the hatch door closed. From somewhere inside the church, old wood groaned, creaking in the wind. Owen looked between the two of them. "Are we leaving, then? We ought to leave."

Guy went back through the doorway. At the place where the roof gaped open, he stopped, staring up as Catherine had at the fractured timber beams and the open sky.

His dark coat was unbuttoned, and his watch chain glinted against his waistcoat. Catherine remembered the complete silence that had enveloped them when he'd made time stand still. There was a similar stillness to him now, his expression thoughtful.

She walked over to him, Owen following her out of the room. Guy raised his lantern, casting his face in light.

"I do wonder," he said, "if perhaps Mr. Carlyle found the

timepiece here after all. Perhaps we missed our chance."

Catherine bit her lip. "I'm going to speak with him tomorrow."

Guy's gaze went to the church entrance. Voice low, he said, "I'm beginning to think this timepiece is not worth finding, if those looking are being killed."

Catherine crossed her arms. The night wind tugged at her coat, strands of her hair loosening from her chignon. "It's magic that brought Mr. Smith back to life. There are people who would take another's life for such a thing."

"Contrary, isn't it?" Turning to Owen, Guy continued. "Someone took your life, Mr. Smith. Then it was restored to you. It's entirely cruel."

"You're assuming," Catherine pointed out, "that the person who killed Mr. Smith is the same person who enchanted the timepiece and that the magic worked as intended. Given our involvement, I suspect it did not."

The three of them made their way out of the church. Walking over the grounds, Owen kept a few paces ahead. He wandered through the rows of tombstones, his head down, his hands in his pockets. Beyond the glow of Guy's light, he looked like a ghost among the graves, a fleeting shadow caught in the corner of one's eye. Something ephemeral.

Catherine glanced to Guy. "The last time I was in Rose Hill Cemetery," she said, voice quiet, "the client didn't pay Mr. Ainsworth with coin but with information. He knew the location of Mr. Smith's plot."

"You're just mentioning this now?"

"It only just came to mind."

Guy adjusted the wick of his lantern, the light flaring brighter. "What was the gentleman's name? Do you remember it?"

"Mr. Geoffrey Watt."

Surprise flickered across his face. "I know him," he said. "He's a past client of my father's. I've seen his name in the books."

"How do you suppose he came across such information?"

Up ahead, Owen had gotten farther from them. He paused, looking back, waiting near the gates.

"I think we have his address noted," said Guy. "Shall we pay him a call?"

Catherine nodded in agreement. They reached Owen where the cemetery gates gave way to the cobbled street, shops shuttered up for the night. He held fast to the iron as he had that night, the last night they were all here together.

"Are you well, Mr. Smith?" Guy asked.

Letting go of the gate, Owen turned to them. He looked little different from the boy they had pulled from the grave, except for the spark that lit his eyes now—recognition and familiarity. "You may call me Owen," he told them. "I think I would prefer it if you did."

Catherine smiled. They journeyed back to the watchmaker's, the way there as recognizable to her as the course to the print shop. In the kitchen, she placed her trunk on the floor near the table, looking it over to ensure all her things were packed away. Owen settled in one of the worn armchairs by the hearth as Guy built up a fire. The wood shifted and popped, and sparks shot upward. In the quiet, Catherine told Owen about Geoffrey Watt—about his knowledge of Owen's grave.

The shop clocks tolled the hour. Owen stretched out his legs in front of him, absently picking at a loose thread on the chair arm. "We ought to visit him, yes. When should we go?" He looked from her to Guy, who now stood at the counter, taking biscuits from a tin and setting them on a plate.

"We could try tomorrow evening," said Catherine. "After I finish work."

Guy brought the biscuits over to the table. Owen got up, yawned, and took two off the plate before heading to bed. Catherine closed her trunk and met Guy's gaze. His eyes were dark in the firelight, his mouth halfway to a smile.

She said softly, "Thank you for letting me stay."

"It was lovely having you here." Looking down at her trunk, he bit his lip. "I can walk with you tomorrow—to the print shop. If you'd like some company."

Catherine felt her cheeks warm. "I'd like that very much."

Guy grinned. It was a grin that lit up his whole face, his eyes shining. Catherine's heart sped at the sight of it, and she grinned back, swift as quicksilver.

CHAPTER TWENTY-ONE

OUTSIDE THE *INVERCARN CHRONICLE*, Catherine and Guy paused on the street. Watery morning light shone across the windows, softening the edges of things. The street glistened with puddles, their surfaces reflecting the pale-gray clouds, the cast-iron lampposts. Catherine looked over at Guy as he put down her trunk and took off his hat. His face was tinged pink by the chill in the air, his expression set as he gazed up at the building.

"I'll be all right," Catherine said, reading the concern on his face.

His eyes met hers. Smiling a little, he replied, "Of course. I have every confidence in you, Catherine."

She picked up her trunk and recalled the first time she'd come here, with her father.

How uncertain she had felt, how decided she had been despite that.

Now here she was with Guy Nolan at her side and the unknown before her.

She said, "I'll pay you a call in the evening," and started for the door.

She'd taken only a few steps, when Guy said, "Catherine, wait."

He caught up to her. And then he paused, clutching his hat in front of him. A carriage passed by on the street, its wheels rolling through the puddles, sending up small waves of rainwater.

Catherine raised her eyebrows in question. "Is evening not a suitable time?"

"No," he said. "I mean—yes, it is. Of course. I only . . . I only wanted to—" He swallowed visibly, his face reddening. "I just wanted to say how much I admire you, Catherine, and—" He stopped again, shutting his eyes tight. "Oh God, I'm sorry. Never mind." Turning on his heel, he began walking quickly away.

Catherine stared after him. The wind blew at his coat, his hair. He put on his hat and dug his hands into his pockets. Picking up her skirts in her free hand, she dashed down the street. Now she was the one calling out. "Guy, wait!"

He looked back around, his expression shy. "Yes?"

Grinning up at him, she smoothed a hand over her coat. "So, you admire me, do you? I'd like to hear the rest."

Guy let out a startled laugh. It was such a lovely sound, and he grinned the way he had last night, with his happiness gleaming in his dark eyes. "My apologies," he said. "I panicked."

"Yes, I gathered." She took a step forward, her smile softening. "Would it ease your mind to know that I also admire you?"

His eyes glistened with tears. He wiped them away, laughing as he did. When she offered him her hand, he held it in both of his. "Stay for dinner tonight, won't you?" he said. "I promise it'll be most entertaining and I'll make wonderful conversation and food and it'll be wonderful."

"Well, that's certainly a promise." She squeezed his fingers. "Of course I will." She let herself gaze at him a moment longer—his windswept hair, the depth of his brown eyes, the curve of his smile—then looked back at the brick and mortar of the print shop. "But for now I must return to work."

Catherine set her completed forme on the bed of the press, wiping her hands on her apron. It was close to afternoon, and through the front windows, the weather looked dull and dreary. The others in the shop were composing type, inking formes, hanging printed sheets to dry. Rather than settle into the routine with ease, Catherine had spent the morning on edge. She knew the source of her discomfort—the memory of Ainsworth's dead body only three floors up, the notion that someone here may be a killer. She inked her forme for printing, her grip tight on the roller.

Time seemed to slow to a crawl. She wouldn't head for the watchmaker's shop until day's end. Boyd came out from the back room, giving them their break early, before heading out on an errand. She hadn't yet seen Spencer, but she had a mind to go upstairs to his room and knock on his door. As Boyd left the shop, she set down her composing stick, her attention shifting to the stairs.

On the third floor, she tapped her knuckles on Spencer's door. "Spencer," she said. "It's Catherine." She put a hand on the door-knob. The rooms on this floor hadn't locks, so she cracked the door open, glancing in. "Spencer?"

Spencer wasn't there. His bed was neatly made, his desk at the window cleared of paper. Catherine took a step inside, looking about the space. If he'd found the timepiece last night, might it be somewhere here?

Crossing the room, she put her fingertips to the desk's edge. She paused, hesitating, her gaze fixed on the street outside. She ought to be checking Boyd's office. If she found some evidence of arsenic there, she could bring it to the police.

She took a deep breath and reached for the first drawer.

A creak in the floorboards told her of someone else's presence.

"Catherine? What are you doing?"

She stilled. Stepping away from Spencer's desk, she turned to find Bridget standing in the hall, regarding her with raised eyebrows. "If Spencer learns you've pried into his things, he'll—"

"I'm not prying," she lied, clasping her hands together. "I'm just—"

From below, the shop door slammed open. Catherine and Bridget looked at each other, equally puzzled, but Catherine's eyes widened as she heard a voice she recognized.

"Miss Daly! Miss Daly, are you here?"

Owen Smith.

"Who is that?" asked Bridget. She followed Catherine back down to the print floor, where they met Owen at the foot of the stairs. He was hatless, his face pale. He put his knuckles to his mouth as though he couldn't bear to speak.

"Owen," Catherine said. "Is something the matter?"

His eyes were dark and red-rimmed. "Please," he said. "You must come at once. Please, Catherine." His voice broke in his distress, catching on a sob.

Catherine placed a hand on his arm, reassuring, even as her heart pounded in her chest. "Of course. It's all right." She looked to Bridget. "Tell Mr. Boyd I'll be back later."

"But—" Bridget shook her head. "Catherine . . ."

Catherine untied her apron, hung it up, and fetched her coat and bonnet.

When she came back downstairs, Owen turned for the door. Out on the street, he wiped at his eyes with his coat sleeve, taking a shuddering breath. He said, "I don't know what to do."

"What's happened? Is it Guy?"

He nodded. "His—his father has died."

Catherine's breath left her in a rush. She recalled with clarity the fondness in Henry Nolan's voice when he'd spoken to Guy, the kindness in his gaze. She did not wish to know how he'd died.

"Guy has not left his bedside," Owen continued. "He won't speak. I told him I'd go and get you—he didn't even seem to hear me."

She couldn't imagine how Guy must feel, losing the only family he had left. They walked quickly back to the watchmaker's shop, and in the gray afternoon light, nothing looked amiss, though the CLOSED sign was hung on the door. Catherine went inside and up the back staircase. The stillness that greeted her in the hall reminded her of the shroud of silence that fell when Guy's magic was at work. Her footsteps were muffled by the carpet runner, her heart pounding in her ears.

Easing open the door, she saw Guy first, kneeling at the side of the bed. His father lay in it, as if he merely slept. The sight brought her back to Ainsworth's office, back to the hospital morgue. She knew what death looked like.

Guy's hand rested on the coverlet. Catherine took it in hers, gently, and he didn't pull away. He tipped his face up, his eyes glazed over with agony. Without saying anything, she led him out of the room.

She closed the door once they were in the hall. Guy sat with his back against the wall, his fingers digging into the carpet runner. At the click of the door closing, his breathing turned shallow.

Small, choked sounds escaped him, and he covered his face with his hands, his shoulders shaking.

Catherine swallowed hard. She touched his shoulder, letting him know she was there. Owen sat on the other side of him, and they waited in that dim and narrow stretch of hallway, while Guy cried into his hands, while Henry Nolan lay dead in the room behind them.

Exhaling shakily, he wiped his face with his shirtsleeve. He pressed his temple to the wallpaper, shutting his eyes.

"Guy," Catherine murmured. "I'm so sorry."

He fixed his gaze on her. And he whispered, "He was murdered, Catherine." Burst capillaries threaded the whites of his eyes, his voice raw and cracked through. "He was murdered. I know it."

Catherine looked over her shoulder at the door. Guy shuddered beside her, continuing in the same half whisper. "The window in his room is unlatched. Someone has been here. Someone poisoned him."

She turned back to him. "You mean," she said softly, "like Mr. Ainsworth?"

He nodded and closed his eyes once more.

Owen said, "We ought to tell the police, oughtn't we?"

They sat in silence for a moment. Guy staggered to his feet, leaning against the wall to steady himself. He didn't look toward his father's bedroom, but concentrated on the floor as he said, "Yes. Yes, we must tell the police." He ran a hand through his hair, glancing over at Catherine. "Then we must visit Mr. Watt."

Catherine stood up. She didn't say what she wanted to—that perhaps she ought to go to Geoffrey Watt's residence by herself. He had information about Owen, surely, but she wondered if Owen could sit through a discussion of his own death. And Guy had just lost his father. He was in no state to be making inquiries about murder.

Guy seemed to read her hesitation. He took a handkerchief from his trouser pocket, wiping again at his tear-stained face, but it didn't alleviate the redness of his eyes, nor the shaking of his hands. "I'm not staying behind, Catherine."

She imagined him sitting alone downstairs while clocks chimed the passing hours. Her throat closed at the thought. "Very well," she said.

"Yes, I'm coming along too," said Owen, getting to his feet. "It's best if we all go. This man knew where I was buried—he might know who killed me."

Guy started down the hall, heading for the stairs. Catherine took another glance at the bedroom door as Owen followed Guy. The floorboards creaked beneath them, the sounds of the clocks in the shop below muffled but steady as a heartbeat. Catherine turned away and set off after them.

CHAPTER TWENTY-TWO

CATHERINE SAT NEXT to Owen as the omnibus rattled over North Bridge. A patchy drizzle speckled the cobbles, the dark evening sky holding the promise of more rain. Leaning against her shoulder, Owen pitched his voice low. "What are we going to do, Catherine?" His gaze went to Guy, sitting on the bench across from them.

Guy had spoken little since leaving the shop. Now he sat with his shoulders slumped, head down, so Catherine couldn't see his face.

Policemen had returned with them to the watchmaker's shop. In the back room, they'd questioned Guy, and he'd stared down at the floor, his voice growing quieter with each answer he gave.

"He was dead when I found him," he'd said. "He took medicine, to help him sleep, but it's not the same sort I saw on his nightstand. It was replaced with something else."

Her heart ached as she remembered Guy's smile that morning, the light in his eyes. To Owen, she said, "He needs time. His father was all the family he had."

Owen looked to the rest of the people crowding the omnibus. Almost every space was occupied, umbrellas folded up and dripping rainwater. He cast his gaze down, skimming his fingers over the brim of his hat.

"What are you thinking, Owen?"

"Only that . . ." He swallowed. "I don't think my memories are going to come back, and I know I likely don't have any family, but—I'm hoping we are friends?"

"Yes." Catherine smiled softly. "Of course we are."

He smiled back at her, his hazel eyes bright. He looked again in Guy's direction, and his smile fell away. "I wish there were some way to ease his pain."

"I wish it too," said Catherine. "We'll help him however we can, but grief isn't a wound that can be neatly stitched."

Owen nodded. They were silent for the remainder of their journey, the omnibus clipping along, passing the establishments that made up the university district. Near Watt's street, the three of them stepped out and started walking. The mansions here were great brick piles, their hedges and gardens leafless this late in the autumn, but Catherine had seen how many flowers bloomed here in the summer months.

Geoffrey Watt resided in a fine two-story house lined with windows. Smoke curled above the chimneys, the white-painted door a stark contrast to the gray evening. Inside, they were shown into a parlor room, and Catherine seated herself in an armchair near the fire. Guy and Owen sat in chairs across from her. The walls were papered in dark red, the furniture heavy and polished. Guy took his pocket watch from his waistcoat, not to mark the time; he merely pressed it against the palm of his hand. The firelight drew attention to the tangle of his hair, the pallor of his countenance. There was a glassiness to his brown eyes that suggested he was somewhere else entirely.

Leaning forward, Catherine said softly, "Guy, you needn't stay here. Perhaps . . ."

He blinked and looked her way, coming back to himself. "Pardon?"

"I said you needn't—"

The parlor door opened. Watt walked in, regarding the three of them. He'd not yet changed for the evening; he wore a fitted frock coat and dark trousers, his cravat tied in a centered bow. Catherine remembered how he'd stood before his sister's grave, melancholy and unsure. He seemed an altogether different man in his own house, surrounded by the elegance of the parlor. He was clearly a little bewildered at their presence, but he welcomed them in all manner of politeness.

"I apologize for keeping you waiting. I assume this is not a social call." He took a seat on the sofa. "Good evening to you, Miss Daly. Mr. Nolan." His eyes caught on Owen. "I don't believe we've met."

Guy cleared his throat. "This is my cousin," he said. "Owen Smith."

"A pleasure," said Watt. "I wasn't aware Henry Nolan had much in the way of family."

"He is a cousin on my mother's side." Guy paused, clutching his pocket watch in a white-knuckled grip. "My father . . . my father passed away earlier today."

"Oh, gracious. I'm sorry, Mr. Nolan."

"Mr. Watt," Catherine said, "we're here because we have questions. You've no doubt heard news of Mr. Ainsworth's death. We've reason to believe both deaths were a result of poisoning."

Watt's eyes widened. He leaned back against the sofa, his hands on his knees. "Well," he said. "Good heavens."

Guy returned his gaze to the fire, saying nothing. Catherine continued. "I know you had information Mr. Ainsworth was seeking—the location of a timepiece. You gave him directions to an unmarked plot in the cemetery, yet when he sent me to retrieve it, there was no such thing to be found."

Watt cast his eyes down. "I didn't think he'd dig up the grave for it."

"He didn't." Catherine gripped the seat of her chair. "I did."

With a sigh, Watt lifted his gaze to meet hers. "I directed him there thinking it would discourage him. The timepiece wasn't left in that coffin." He looked over at Guy, his brow creased. "I imagine it's still in your shop, Mr. Nolan."

Catherine turned to Guy in confusion. He didn't move; he seemed not to have heard, but slowly, voice rasping, he said, "Why would it be there?"

In the chair next to him, Owen regarded Watt with a fearful expression, hopeful and morbidly curious. "The boy in the grave," he began, "do you know who killed him, sir?"

Watt swallowed. "I would prefer not to speak on it."

"You do yourself no favors that way, Mr. Watt," said Catherine. "How did you come to know these things? Why would the time-piece be in Mr. Nolan's shop?"

"Because it belonged to him. Henry Nolan."

Guy's attention snapped to Watt. Catherine had seen the bleak-ness in his eyes, but in that moment it was the darkness of a storm rolling in.

"You must understand I only learned of this recently," Watt went on. "In the summer, my father told it to me on his deathbed. He said Mr. Nolan gave him the pocket watch about fifteen years ago. He said the man was grieved, having just lost his wife and two sons. Mr. Nolan asked if there was some way to keep his third son safe—if illness or accident were to take his life, if he might be able to restore it." Watt hesitated, biting his lip. To Guy, he said, "I know your family's magic, Mr. Nolan. You might still time, but not wind it back. Your father knew there was only so much his magic could do to achieve what he wanted. My father agreed to help him, but magic—especially on that scale—it isn't easily done, and it isn't done without cost."

Catherine was all too aware of the fact. She knew what must've come about all those years ago. She said, "One would need to take a life in order to give life to another."

Watt nodded. "He was a foundling boy. My father made sure of that. He killed him quickly."

Guy's expression was so thunderous, Catherine thought he might take Watt by the lapels and shake him. She fairly wanted to do just that. His voice held a hard undercurrent as he said, "Do not justify it so, Mr. Watt. It was murder."

"Yes, that was your father's sentiment when my father returned the timepiece to him with the magic he'd asked for within it. A life for a life. Mr. Nolan was none too pleased, and rightfully so, I suppose. But . . . Surely in his heart of hearts he must've known what it would take?"

The conversation Catherine had overheard between Guy and Everley returned to the forefront of her thoughts.

Mr. Everley. You don't think I'd ever use it, do you?

No. I only fear your father might.

Guy got up, walking out of the room, and Catherine released a sigh. She looked to Owen, pressed back against the armchair opposite her. His face was white as paper. "Come, Owen." She kept her voice gentle. "I think we've heard enough."

At the doorway, she paused with her hand on the frame. "Mr. Watt," she said, "do you happen to know what this timepiece looks like?"

"Indeed." He went over to a writing desk in the corner, lifting the rosewood lid. "I hoped to speak with Mr. Nolan about it, a few months ago, but he seemed to no longer remember it. I fear the guilt might've led him to recklessness—I heard he'd been selling pieces of time for a while. Such business would've eaten away at his memories." Sitting at the desk, he picked up a pencil and began to sketch. "The watch Henry Nolan gave my father was a lovely silver piece. My father had it for a little time before he—well, before he gave it back to Mr. Nolan."

Finishing his sketch of the timepiece, Watt handed the paper to Catherine. "That timepiece holds powerful magic. Someone from the *Chronicle*—Mr. Carlyle—was asking me about it only recently. He knew I misled Mr. Ainsworth regarding its whereabouts. I told him it might still be in the Nolans' shop, but I couldn't be entirely sure. Mr. Nolan would do well to find it."

Catherine looked down at the timepiece Watt had drawn. She swallowed against the tightness in her throat, and Watt's words echoed in her mind as she and Owen left the parlor.

Outside, Guy stood in the front courtyard. It was raining quite steadily now, and the shoulder cape of his overcoat was soaked through. He looked over at the sound of their footsteps. Owen began to say something, but then Guy put his arms around him. And despite being pressed against the wet wool of Guy's coat, Owen leaned in gratefully.

"It was vile what he said," Guy told him. "Your life isn't worth any less than mine. My father oughtn't have—" His voice turned choked. "I'm so sorry. You died because of—"

Owen managed to free one of his arms to pat Guy on the back. "Do not think it your fault. It wasn't, Guy. It wasn't."

"Guy," said Catherine. She held out the bit of paper. "Have a look at this."

He stepped back from Owen, taking his reading glasses from his pocket. Raindrops dotted the paper as Guy studied the picture of the timepiece. "Dear God." He shook his head. "To think, all this time . . ."

"So you know where it is?" Owen asked.

"It's the pocket watch I was wearing . . . the night Catherine and I dug up your grave." Guy looked up from Watt's sketch. "In fact, the crystal over the face broke. I thought it was so old, I must've cracked it while we were digging. I left it on the worktable. I've been meaning to repair it."

Yet Catherine felt a creeping dread rather than any sense of relief. She started across the courtyard, rain slipping down past her collar, making her shiver. She said, "Let's hope it's still there."

The omnibus ride back to the watchmaker's shop was a long one. They got off, and though the streetlights illuminated the way, no lamps burned inside the shop. Guy reached into his pocket for his key, gazing up at the curtained windows of the flat. Catherine's heart clenched.

He went inside and began lighting the lamps. The shop glowed with warmth, all dark wood and clockwork, the smell of polish and metal. Catherine took off her coat and bonnet, setting them on the coatrack.

Guy paused at the doorway to the back room. Catherine came to stand beside him. Only yesterday, Guy had sat at the worktable while his father looked over his shoulder, advising him. Now he stared into the dimness of the room, his expression achingly vulnerable.

He took a breath and stepped inside, lighting the desk lamp. There were several pocket watches on the table—in movement holders, gears exposed, or still in their casings—but after a fleeting glance, Guy said, "It's not here." He bent down, opening drawers.

"Unless my father moved it, but I doubt that."

Inside the drawers, there were more tools, tarnished pocket watches and chains, rusted gears, fragments of metal.

Owen's voice wavered. "How will we find it?"

Guy's shoulders sagged as he looked back at him. "Whoever killed my father—I imagine they have it now." He closed his eyes and pressed the heels of his palms against them.

Catherine said, "So we'll find them," and her manner was just as resolute as Guy had been on noting the timepiece's absence. "Mr. Nolan was killed in the same manner as Mr. Ainsworth. The medical examiner told the police about Mr. Ainsworth being poisoned. Someone at the print shop has done this."

Her thoughts turned to Spencer wandering the cemetery in the night, asking about the timepiece at the university. He'd been absent from the print shop earlier today, but then so had Boyd, taking off on an errand. She ought to return and see if they were there now, but she couldn't find the will to leave. In all likelihood, someone at the print shop had poisoned Ainsworth, poisoned Henry Nolan, and stolen the timepiece to use for their own ends.

Later in the evening, Catherine turned down the light of the desk lamp and slipped beneath the blankets on the sofa. The ticking of the clocks provided a small comfort, a reminder of previous nights, happier ones.

She awoke to the same near darkness. Her head was clouded with sleep, and she was momentarily unsure what had woken her. Then footsteps sounded above. Someone else was awake—moving around in the kitchen. Catherine stared bleary-eyed at the ceiling, worry gnawing at her insides. A chair scraped against the floor, muffled but distinct. She sat up and reached for her clothes, dressing quickly in the dim.

A clock behind the shop counter displayed the early-morning

hour. Its golden pendulum swung side to side, rhythmic, as she crossed the floor in her stockinged feet. The mechanism chimed the hour in doleful tones along with the rest, the sound following her as she started up the stairs.

In the kitchen, Guy sat at the table with a candle offering feeble light. When she came to the doorway, he looked over to meet her gaze. Catherine couldn't tell if he'd woken from some terrible nightmare or simply hadn't slept at all. His eyes were red and fever-bright, the collar of his nightshirt damp with sweat. "Did I wake you?" His voice came out hoarse. "I'm sorry."

Catherine stopped just inside the room. She felt as though she could go no farther. "I can go back downstairs, if you'd like to be alone."

He shook his head. She took a seat across from him and realized he was crying, silently, the tears slipping down his face as he blinked. He wiped them away with his knuckles. When his hands came to rest atop the table, Catherine curled her own around them, squeezing lightly.

"What am I supposed to do now?" he asked. "I don't . . . I don't know what to do."

"I don't know, either, Guy," she said softly. "But I know you needn't figure it out right now."

He bowed his head, a sob escaping him. "This shouldn't have happened. This wasn't supposed to happen." His voice choked. "Owen and my father—my father never should've—" He tipped his head back, blinking up at the ceiling. "You were going to come to dinner."

Catherine whispered, "I'm here now."

He looked at her. Closing his eyes, he took deep breaths. And after a moment, he asked, "Should we go to the print shop tomorrow?"

Catherine swallowed, thinking over the past few days. She recalled Spencer standing beside her in Ainsworth's office. She remembered the pallor of his face and the shaking of his hands as he'd looked upon Ainsworth's body. She imagined him poisoning Ainsworth's tea with arsenic, switching out Henry's medicine, taking the timepiece from the worktable and stepping back out onto the street.

He could be a murderer.

"Let me go with you," said Guy. "We can search for evidence."

"I don't see how we'll manage that, with everyone else there. I tried to have a look around Mr. Carlyle's room today, but my roommate caught me at it."

Guy held on to her hands. His eyes were dark and steady in the candlelight. "We can manage it," he said. "I'll still time, and we can manage it."

Catherine looked back at him. It seemed an easy answer in the quiet of the kitchen. At this hour of the night, time was dreamlike; she could imagine them existing outside the bounds of it already, without consequence.

"Only if you're certain," she told him.

Guy nodded. He drew away from her, his gaze lowered. "What my father did," he started, voice quiet, "I can't bear it, Catherine."

"He wasn't the one who killed Owen."

"Perhaps he didn't hold the knife, but Mr. Watt was right in that he must've known—he must've realized the cost. Now he's gone, and I can't even speak to him of it. He kept selling hours, not telling me why. I never would've thought he did so to forget." Guy stared at the candle flame between them. "Every time I think on it," he whispered, "it hurts to breathe, like I've a shard of ice in my chest."

"You are grieving." Catherine folded her arms on the table and tipped her head to the side. "And you've a kind heart. You know what is good and right in the world."

Guy's mouth quirked. His eyes shone with unshed tears. "At the moment, I feel I do not know much of anything."

From down the hall, a door cracked open. The floorboards creaked under footsteps, and Owen appeared in the kitchen doorway, scratching the back of his head. "What are you two doing?" he asked. "It's very late."

Guy scrubbed the tears from his eyes. He stood up and pressed his hands against the table. "Catherine and I are going to the print shop tomorrow."

Owen regarded them. "Will you be all right?"

Catherine rose from her chair, the candlelight flickering in her wake. She didn't want to think Spencer capable of murder, to think he'd poisoned Henry Nolan and stolen the timepiece, but she was thinking it. "It shouldn't take long," she said. "I believe I know where to look."

CHAPTER TWENTY-THREE

ONCE IT WAS PROPERLY morning and sunlight shone in through the windows, Catherine joined Guy and Owen in the kitchen for breakfast. The table was taken up with plates of toast and eggs, teacups and saucers between them.

After she'd sat down, Owen said, "I've been thinking over this plan of yours and I've decided I do not like it one jot."

Guy turned a page of his newspaper. He said, "It's a fine plan. And we're doing it. We're only having a look around. The police ought to be scouring the place." He shifted his gaze to Catherine and offered her a smile. Like Owen, he was neatly dressed. His dark cravat was tied sharply, his waistcoat free of wrinkles. His eyes were a little clearer, not as haunted as they had looked in the night. "Good morning, Catherine."

"Good morning." She poured herself a cup of tea, adding milk to it.

Owen said, "This person is a murderer. You need to be careful."

"We'll be safe as houses," Guy replied. "No one will even know we're there. I'll hold time still long enough for us to search properly. If we find the arsenic used, or the timepiece, we can bring them to the police."

Owen ducked his head, staring into his teacup. He hadn't touched it, and from what Catherine could tell, he hadn't eaten anything, either. "But what if you don't come back?" His voice was a half whisper. "What if something happens?"

"Oh, Owen," said Catherine, not unkindly. "Nothing will happen."

Guy took off his glasses and rubbed a hand over his eyes.

"Perhaps I should come with you." Owen swallowed, fidgeting with a handkerchief on the table. "I could help."

"No." Guy's tone brooked no argument. "If you come along, you're one more person I have to extend my magic over. The fewer people there, the better."

In the back room, he found a watch to use, marking the case with a spot of his blood and fitting in the winding key. Catherine watched as he wound it, but it wasn't like before. Guy took out the key, and time halted—then continued on. He wound the watch again. Once everything was still, Guy looked to her, his eyes glassy with tiredness.

"How long do we have?" she asked.

"Two hours." The watch slipped from his grasp, landing on the floor with a thud, and he pressed the heel of his hand against his forehead as Catherine moved to pick it up. "That ought to be enough time, yes?"

"Are you well?"

He closed his eyes. "I feel strange."

Catherine reached out, taking his hand. "You should've gotten more rest. Are you sure you want to do this?"

Guy nodded tightly. The memory of the last time he'd used his magic hung between them unsaid. Out on the street, Catherine tried not to look too closely at those she passed, fixed as they were midstep, suspended in a single moment. As they turned the corner, the print shop just ahead, Guy faltered.

"Catherine," he said. "What if there's nothing to find?"

If there was nothing to find, then Guy had lost memories to no purpose. His face was pale, and he was shaking as if he were cold, though the wind remained still along with everything else.

"We'll find something. I know it." And she hoped by saying so, she made it true.

The way to the *Chronicle* was murky with fog, heavy with silence. Catherine could usually hear the wash of the river this close to it, but the tide was unmoving, boats stationary in the water.

She opened the door to the print shop and stepped inside.

Across the way, she saw Bridget at her desk, alongside others she knew. Their heads were bent, hands motionless around composing sticks, fingers paused in the act of reaching for type. Catherine glanced over at Guy. He closed the door slowly, his tone uncertain as he said, "Where do we look first?"

"Upstairs." She bit her lip. "Are you all right?"

He nodded without meeting her gaze. She made out a muffled ticking, and Guy drew his pocket watch from his waistcoat. It was still counting down the minutes, the time that continued to elapse for them.

"Mr. Carlyle's room is on the third floor," she told him.

They started upstairs, and in the timeless silence, Catherine was all too aware of her own footfalls, the creak of each step, the pounding of her heart. They came to Spencer's door, and she opened it, only to find the room empty.

"Oh, good," said Guy. "He's not here."

Catherine shook her head. "The timepiece could be on his person."

"Might he be somewhere else in the building?"

"Perhaps. I didn't notice him on the print floor."

He must've returned here sometime in her absence—where his desk was clear the day before, now there were papers across it, a few pens, a pot of ink, alongside one of Ainsworth's ledgers. Catherine flipped it open, paging through it.

Guy opened a cabinet and surveyed its sparse contents. There were knickknacks, but no watches. Looking back at the desk, Catherine pulled open the first drawer.

Envelopes, paper for correspondence. She tried the second, but the timepiece wasn't there, either. Fear crept into her heart. What if someone else had it? Someone they hadn't considered.

In the third drawer, she found a plain vial, half full, a cork stopper in place. She lifted it out carefully and showed it to Guy. The label had been torn, but Catherine didn't need one, for what she also found in the drawer was a timepiece, the crystal cracked across the front. It was an old pocket watch, tarnished silver. She took hold of it and brought it out into the light.

"Yes," said Guy. "That's it."

And then he frowned. Removing the watch from his own pocket, he stared down at the face of it, a crease marking his brow. He snapped his attention to the window. "Oh dear."

An instant later, Catherine understood his alarm. The distinct clatter of the presses echoed up from the print floor, work continuing downstairs. The stillness of Guy's magic had fallen away, and Catherine recalled the way time jarred to a halt before carrying on at the watchmaker's shop.

"I can wind it again," said Guy. "I can—it won't take a moment." He dug into his pocket, presumably in search of the winding key.

Out in the hall, the stairs groaned under footsteps.

They hadn't even thought to close the door.

"Guy," Catherine said, and it was a whisper, a breath.

He looked back at her, the panic in his eyes clear as glass. "Let's leave," he said. "We can just—"

Spencer Carlyle appeared in the doorway. He paused at the sight of them, blinking, bringing one hand to rest on the frame. Stepping inside, he closed the door behind him. He took care doing so, but he may as well have slammed it shut, the way Catherine's pulse jumped.

His voice was careful too.

"Catherine." His gaze flickered over her, before landing on Guy. "Mr. Nolan. What are you doing in here?"

Catherine gripped the vial, the pocket watch clutched in her other hand. She showed the vial to Spencer, trying her best to keep her voice steady as she asked, "Why do you have this?"

Spencer let out a weary sigh. "Catherine—"

"You poisoned Mr. Nolan? Mr. Ainsworth?"

He regarded her, a dangerous shine to his blue eyes. Tipping his chin in Guy's direction, he said, "Did he tell you that timepiece belonged to his father? A boy was killed to work its magic, and Mr. Nolan let it happen."

Beside her, Guy flinched.

"He didn't know," said Catherine softly. "He didn't know until it was done. We only learned of it recently." She put the timepiece and the vial away in her coat pocket, not taking her eyes off

Spencer. "You stole it from Mr. Nolan's shop, didn't you? Why?"

Spencer didn't answer at once. He stood blocking the way to the door, and all Catherine could think was:

How are we to get out?

"That timepiece is valuable, Catherine. Mr. Ainsworth made a bit of coin from the farewell service, but this—this magic—is what people truly want. How much would someone pay to bring those dearest to them back to life?"

Catherine took a shuddering breath, chancing a look over at Guy. His face was ashen, and in his stillness he seemed almost fixed in place by his own magic, one of his hands still tucked in the pocket of his coat.

"Spencer," Catherine said, turning back. "You need to let us leave."

"Need to?" He raised his eyebrows. "Ah, yes, so you may take the timepiece and do whatever you please with it."

Her jaw clenched. For two years, she'd lived under the same roof as him, spoke with him as easily as her fellow printers. She did not know how to align the Spencer she knew with the one standing before her now. "I'm not giving it to you," she said. "No one ought to use it."

"Catherine." He extended a hand, palm up. "I can't let you leave. I can't let either of you leave. I know you well enough to know you'll take this to the police."

"You killed two people, Spencer."

He stepped closer, and Catherine drew back, pressing up against the desk.

"Mr. Carlyle," said Guy. His breathing was a little short, but his voice held firm. "You cannot . . . You cannot kill us in this room. It would be too difficult to hide our bodies. We'll leave the watch and the vial. We'll take no evidence."

Catherine stared, wide-eyed. *How could they do such a thing?*

But then Spencer said, "I can't take that chance. You know what I've done."

Guy didn't waver. He held Spencer's gaze and told him, "My magic could be of use to you." His voice was quiet, serious. "Let Miss Daly leave, and I'll give you time to gather your things and go." From his pocket, he took out his watch and winding key.

Spencer considered him. Catherine curled her fingers around the desk's edge, unsure of what Guy was doing. She looked over, but his eyes remained fixed on Spencer. He slotted the key into the watch and continued. "It's a fine offer, Mr. Carlyle. You'd do well to take it."

Eyes narrowed, Spencer said, "It's a fine offer, indeed. But I don't know you, Mr. Nolan. How am I to trust you'll keep your word?"

And, finally, in that moment, Guy's eyes flitted to Catherine. His grip tightened around his watch and key, and she realized what he meant to do. Glancing back at Spencer, he said grimly, "I suppose you can't."

He closed his eyes. He wound the watch at a swift pace, his magic unfolding—until silence fell, settling like a sudden frost.

Spencer stood just as he was. His eyes were wide, his mouth open as though he were caught midprotest.

Guy let out a breath of laughter. He stumbled back a step and knelt, clutching his watch to his chest. He looked to Catherine with a grin, tears shining in his eyes. "I wasn't sure that would work."

"Oh, Guy."

He scrubbed at his tears with the back of one hand. "Do you have the timepiece?"

She nodded. Pulling herself away from the desk, she took out the pocket watch. It was an ordinary, dull silver, its casing scratched.

Guy straightened up. "And what about Mr. Carlyle?"

They looked over at him. Despite his still expression, there was a harshness to it, a stark light in his pale gaze.

"I believe there's some rope in the kitchen," said Catherine. "We can restrain him."

She stepped out into the hall, Guy following just behind. He shut the door, and at the click of the bolt, the finality of it, Catherine's breath caught in her throat. She put her arms around him, and he leaned his head upon her shoulder, holding on to her. She felt him shaking, the rapid beat of his heart. Tears stung the backs of her eyes.

Guy whispered, "Are you all right?"

"Yes." And though it was the truth, she choked on the word. "Are you?"

"I'm fine."

Catherine supposed they hadn't much time, but Guy said nothing of it. The two of them stood, embracing each other in the dimly lit hall, quiet, everything around them still.

CHAPTER TWENTY-FOUR

TIME RECOMMENCED JUST before they reached the police station. Guy leaned against the building, his eyes drifting shut, the shadows beneath them noticeable. They blinked open when Catherine took his hand.

"Come," she said. "We can't stand out here in the cold."

Inside, there was a lobby wallpapered in dark green. A line of chairs was set against the wall, thin-cushioned and hard-backed, but Guy dropped into one without complaint, resting his chin in the palm of his hand, closing his eyes again.

Catherine said softly, "I'll speak with the police, Guy. You wait here, all right?"

When he made no reply, she realized he'd fallen asleep.

The secretary at the desk directed her to a detective sergeant, who sent out a few constables to collect Spencer at the print shop.

He then led her down a dimly lit hallway, into his office, where she sat in an armchair across from his desk.

She told him the whole of the situation. She spoke haltingly, her voice sounding too high to her ears, but the sergeant remained patient as she explained. The task Mr. Ainsworth had given her, the suddenness of his death, followed by Henry Nolan's, and her suspicion of Spencer Carlyle. She continued on, telling him how she and Guy had found the timepiece in Spencer's room, along with the vial of arsenic. She set the vial on his desk. It rolled a little, the substance inside shifting.

The sergeant clasped his hands atop his desk. His side-whiskers were trimmed neatly, his face pale and haggard in the lamplight. His dark eyes watched the vial of arsenic tip back and forth until it settled. "Miss Daly," he said, "you should've come to us with this sooner, rather than put yourselves in harm's way. We were aware of the arsenic poisoning in Mr. Ainsworth's case, as with Mr. Nolan's."

"Yes, sir." Truly, she wasn't sure what else to say. Any argument she made would do her no favors.

The sergeant let out a sigh, rubbing at the lines across his forehead. "All right, Miss Daly. Thank you. I suggest you attend to Mr. Nolan now."

Catherine nodded and hurried out of the room, returning to the lobby. Guy was awake, sitting up, and he smiled when he caught sight of her.

"I still have the timepiece," she told him. "The sergeant didn't ask for it."

She passed it to him. He handled it with the utmost care, tucking it away in his coat.

She continued. "I gave him the vial of arsenic. He's sent some constables to fetch Mr. Carlyle."

Guy got to his feet, dusting himself off. "If they don't need anything else, let's be on our way. I'd rather not be here when they bring Mr. Carlyle in." He made for the door, and out on the street, he held his arm out for her. "You were incredibly brave back there, Catherine."

"As were you."

Guy blushed. He said, "Well, I suppose," and glanced over at the front window of the police station.

Catherine caught sight of her own reflection in the glass. There was nothing about her countenance to show she'd just faced a killer and escaped.

As they started in the direction of the watchmaker's shop, Guy took out the timepiece. It was as Catherine had seen it in Spencer's room, the pale silver flashing in the sunlight. "It's empty," said Guy. "I didn't notice before, but I can feel the difference—there's no magic left. Everyone thought this timepiece could bring back the dead when there was only ever enough magic for one life." Placing the watch in his pocket, he let out a shaky breath. "I'm glad it was given back to Owen—it never should've been taken from him."

They came to the shop, the CLOSED sign propped up in the door, the lamps inside burning low. Catherine felt a rush of relief at the sight of it, overwhelmed that they'd made it here. When they entered, Owen rushed out from the back room. "Oh, thank goodness," he said. "What happened?"

Guy removed the timepiece from his coat. "Well, we've got this."

Owen swallowed. When Guy passed him the watch, he turned it over in his hand, holding it a little away from himself. Giving it back, he said, "It's true, then? Mr. Carlyle—did he—"

"Yes," said Catherine. "We've just come from the police station."

Guy put aside his coat and hat before heading into the back room. Catherine and Owen followed, taking a seat on the sofa; Guy closed the door and sat down at the desk. The shop was quiet as it ever was—the sound of the clocks beyond the door accentuating the silence between the three of them.

It was Owen who spoke first. "I'm glad you're both all right," he said in a whisper. "I sat here all the while, waiting. Whatever we do with the timepiece, it matters not to me—I'm just glad you're back safely."

Catherine untied her bonnet and held it in her lap. She thought Guy ought to be resting after all the magic he'd done, but he seemed quite set on considering the timepiece. He placed his magnifier on his glasses, located a movement holder and the needle-fine tools he required.

"No one will be using the timepiece for anything," said Guy. "There's no magic to it anymore." He set the watch into the movement holder, removing the cracked crystal from the face. "It was used up the moment you awoke from the grave, Owen."

Owen ducked his head to stare down at his hands. "Mr. Carlyle did it all for naught then—poisoning Mr. Nolan and Mr. Ainsworth."

Guy took off his spectacles. He set his eyes on the opposite wall, not looking at either of them. He said simply, "Yes."

Owen made a soft, choked sound that pierced Catherine's heart like an arrow. He said again, "I'm glad you're all right," and brought his knees to his chest, pressing his face against the fold of his arms. "I'm just glad you're all right."

Guy put the timepiece to one side of the desk, his movements slow and careful. Catherine got up from the sofa, standing beside his chair. The tools for watch repair were spaced neatly across the desk's polished surface. In her mind's eye, she saw her desk at the print shop—type in compartments of the case, the handwritten notes, her composing stick. She asked, "What shall we do with it?"

"I'll keep it here," replied Guy. "If the police come asking for it, they can have it." He turned toward her, and she remembered his exhaustion, sitting in the station's lobby.

She said, "I know what you did at the print shop wasn't easy."

He reached for her hand, his expression open and honest. "No, I can't say it was, but it was no simple task for you, either, Catherine. And we did it nevertheless."

CHAPTER TWENTY-FIVE

THAT NIGHT, Catherine sat awake in the back room, looking over the timepiece in the dim lamplight. So many had searched for it, wished for it. All this time, the life it held had already been given back to the person it was taken from.

She placed the timepiece on the worktable and turned down the lamp even further, so there was only a wisp of light to guide her back to the sofa. She was unsure of what tomorrow would bring. With Spencer in police custody, the print shop would be short of a foreman. She'd return there and continue her work. She couldn't linger forever in the watchmaker's shop. She had to choose a path to take—just as she had when she'd left home.

Tugging the blankets up around her shoulders, she listened to the steady ticking of the shop clocks. She knew what she wanted. She saw it when she closed her eyes, clear as day: her small room above the print shop, the clatter of the presses, the smell of paper and ink. She let her eyes slip shut, wishing and hoping as she drifted off to sleep.

It was early in the morning when she was pulled awake to sounds beyond the closed door. Guy, she thought, arranging things in the shop, in preparation for the day. She dressed quickly and opened the door to find him dusting the clocks behind the counter. He turned, cloth in hand. His glasses slid down his nose, and he pushed them up, smiling as he did.

"Good morning, Catherine. Did you sleep well?"

"Yes." She clasped her hands in front of her. "Though you did wake me."

Guy's smile widened. He looked in good health compared to yesterday, his eyes clear behind his spectacles. "Owen is in the kitchen," he said, setting down his cloth and coming around the side of the counter. "And there's tea and toast for you on the table."

Catherine made for the stairs, washed up with water from the ewer, returning back down when she heard a sharp knock at the door. Guy came out of the back room, his expression puzzled as he started across the shop to answer it.

Sydney Mallory stood on the step, holding a bundle of papers. "Hello, Guy." He stepped past him nimbly, doffing his hat. He looked for all the world as though he were here on invitation. "Morning, Miss Daly."

Guy closed the door, regarding Sydney with a wary expression. "What brings you here?"

"I came to speak with Mr. Smith." Sydney walked up to the shop counter, peering into the back room. "I've a gift for him. Where is he?"

"I don't imagine he wants anything of yours," Catherine put in.

"It's not mine," said Sydney in an injured tone. "Rather, it's something of his. You may pass it on to him if he doesn't wish to see me. I can understand why, but I'm here to offer an apology." He waved the papers he held. "And I've brought him this as a testament to my good character."

Guy heaved a sigh. "I'll ask him if he'd like to come down."

Sydney put the papers on the counter as Guy started up the back staircase. He hung up his coat and hat on the rack near the door. Catherine asked him, "Are you still digging up bodies?"

He raised his eyebrows. "No. In fact, I've gotten an apprenticeship at the butcher's. It's why I'm here so early—I've my shift to get to."

Catherine blinked in surprise. She hadn't thought he'd give up the grave work, but perhaps Guy's averseness had swayed him from it. "Well," she said. "I'm glad for you. Do you enjoy it?"

"It's good pay and respectable—and better than unearthing cadavers."

The staircase creaked under footsteps, and Catherine and Sydney looked over. Owen followed after Guy into the shop, his countenance pale. He crossed his arms, aiming a level look at Sydney. "Good morning, Mr. Mallory," he said, and his voice was as stiff as Catherine had ever heard it. "You wished to speak with me?"

"Indeed." Sydney rubbed the back of his neck. "I've come to apologize. I was wrong to frighten you as I did. I'm truly sorry. I—I've brought something you might be interested in." He gathered the papers, offering them up to Owen.

Guy frowned and took his spectacles from his waistcoat pocket.

When Owen made no move forward, Sydney said, "It's from the Boys' Home, Mr. Smith. Your orphanage record. And the name they gave you, if you want it."

"I'm happy with the name I have, thank you." But he reached for the papers and held them to his chest. "Are you certain it's my record?"

Sydney nodded. He looked to Guy and said, "When I came by the other day with your payment, you mentioned Mr. Smith was once an apprentice at the coffin shop on Burnside Lane." He turned back to Owen. "That record says the same—where you were apprenticed after you left the orphanage."

Guy narrowed his eyes. "You didn't come across this record by chance, I assume."

"I stole it, if you must know."

"Sydney." Guy took off his glasses. He pointed them at him, continuing on. "What if you were caught? You can't go around—"

"It belongs to him," said Sydney. "I'm simply giving him what's his. Mr. Smith, would you prefer I take it back to the orphanage?"

Owen shook his head. Sydney looked back at Guy with a radiant smile. "You see, Guy?"

Catherine went to Owen's side. He still had the papers pressed to his shirtfront, his arms wrapped around them. She leaned close as Guy and Sydney carried on talking and asked, "Aren't you going to read it?"

He swallowed hard. "I must confess I'm nervous to. I know already I haven't any family. A foundling, Mr. Watt said I was, but I don't remember that person—the person I was before I died." He bit his lip, before holding the papers out. "Will you keep it for me, Catherine? Until I'm ready to read it? I'd consider it a great favor."

It warmed her heart that he had such trust in her. She accepted the record with care. "Of course." She smiled. "Whenever you're ready."

A little while later, the four of them sat together in the kitchen. Catherine and Guy took turns telling Sydney of yesterday's events, the ensuing somberness in the air broken only by Guy getting up to stoke the fire and brew more tea.

Owen's record remained closed on the table. Catherine looked to it as the discussion moved on to Sydney's new apprenticeship. Owen spent the time staring into his teacup. Once Sydney left and Guy went downstairs to work in the back room, Catherine said, "Don't fret, Owen. We'll go out today, you and me. You'll make a fine apprentice at any trade."

He said nothing to this, but when she stood up from the table, he dutifully followed her. In the hall, he tied his cravat in the looking glass, and in the shop, he made sure his hair lay flat in the shine of a long-case clock. Catherine took his coat from the rack, dusted it off before passing it to him. He put on his hat, and she saw it didn't sit at too rakish an angle.

"There," she said. "You look the perfect gentleman."

He looked very young—his hazel eyes round, his hands soft and clean and without calluses—but then, most apprentices were young.

Guy appeared in the doorway of the back room. "Are you two off somewhere?"

"Yes," said Catherine. "We're to find Owen an apprenticeship by day's end."

This was not met with the reaction she'd expected. The look in Guy's eyes turned dull and distant. "Oh," he said. "Very well." His shoulders slumped. "I only thought—I thought you might like to work here, Owen. I don't yet know all that my father did, but I can still teach you. And I could do with an assistant now that—now that he's gone."

Owen removed his hat. "Work with you?"

"Yes," said Guy firmly. "If you'd like. You've already got a room here, after all."

Owen's eyes glimmered with tears, with hope. He clutched the brim of his hat. "I would like that." He wiped at his eyes, his smile bright and watery. "I really would."

"Then it's decided." Guy walked over, took Owen's hat and placed it back on the coatrack. "You'll stay here with me."

Owen laughed, the sound catching in his throat, and Guy produced a handkerchief, handing it to him. "Come now, Owen," he said gently. "You're all right, aren't you?"

"Yes." Owen smiled through his tears. "I'm all right."

The bell above the shop door rang out. A customer walked in, and Catherine ushered Owen into the back room. He sat down at Guy's worktable as she pulled the door closed. She lit the lamp there, light glowing through the green shade. It shone over the tools and loose watch parts, the small nicks and scratches in the aged wood.

"Not too morbid for you, is it?" she asked.

He ran his fingers along the desk's edge, considering the items before him. "Catherine," he said, solemn in comparison to her lightheartedness. "What about you? Will you go back to the print shop?"

She nodded. "I'd like to. I can't imagine Mr. Boyd liked hearing about Guy and I going through the place while time was stilled. Hopefully I haven't lost my place there again."

"I'm certain you haven't." He regarded her, his eyes luminous. "You and Guy have been so good and kind to me. I can't ever repay you for all you've done."

"Owen Smith, we are your friends."

He reached over and clasped her hand. "Thank you, then, for being a wonderful friend."

Guy entered the room holding a pocket watch. He set it on the worktable and rolled up his shirtsleeves. Owen moved to stand up from the chair, but Guy shook his head. "Listen and look closely, Owen," he said. "This is the first day of your apprenticeship."

Catherine readied herself to depart. She located her coat, her bonnet and gloves, and lingered near the door. Rain tapped at the window glass. She tucked Owen's record away in her coat and took the umbrella Guy offered her.

Casting his gaze down, he said, "You know you're always welcome back here, if you've any trouble."

"Don't say it like a goodbye." Though her throat tightened and tears pricked the backs of her eyes. It felt like a goodbye, even when it wasn't. "I'll come to call tomorrow as soon as I have a chance."

"Yes." Guy looked up in earnest. "Yes, please do. I imagine . . . That is, the police might . . ." He put his arms about himself. "My father's funeral—I haven't had a moment to prepare."

She brought a hand to his cheek. "Give yourself the time you need."

Guy swallowed. The rain picked up, streaking the glass, the street outside becoming a misty blur of gray stone and weathered shopfronts. He said, "Wait here, won't you? Until the rain lets up."

And because he asked, she did.

CHAPTER TWENTY-SIX

IN THE QUIET of the print shop, Catherine wondered if it was the last time she'd set foot here. She rested a hand on one of the presses, the iron cool and familiar beneath her touch. The aprons were still hung on their hooks. The type drawers and pots of ink were put away. It was everything as it should be; Catherine wasn't sure what else she expected.

How badly she wanted to stay.

On the third floor, she paused outside her room. Lamplight glowed beneath the door's edge, though it was still quite early. She stepped inside and found Bridget sitting at the desk, already dressed for the day.

She turned, offering up a smile. "Catherine. It's good to see you."

"I suppose you've heard what happened."

"Yes." Bridget stood up from the desk. Light from the lamp

turned her fair hair golden, shining over the wallpaper behind her. "The police were here most of yesterday. They told us about Spencer—about the timepiece—"

"The magic is gone. It's only an ordinary pocket watch." Catherine sat on the edge of her bed, looking about the room. Quietly, she asked, "How did Mr. Boyd take it? Is he angry with me?"

"No, indeed. Though he'll probably want to speak with you about it."

She felt the press of Owen's record, secure inside her coat. After Bridget left to head downstairs, Catherine knelt at her bedside, pulling out the box beneath it. She set the orphanage papers carefully inside, among her reminders of her family home. It was still home to her, but then, the city had become her home as well.

Catherine put on a clean dress and pinned her dark hair into a chignon. She buttoned her cuffs and smoothed down her skirts. She did a quick study of herself in the looking glass above the washstand, the light coming in through the window catching in her blue eyes. Taking a breath, she started downstairs, waiting at her desk on the shop floor.

She didn't have to wait long.

Mr. Boyd walked into the shop wearing a wool overcoat, which he hung on the rack alongside his silk hat.

"Good morning, sir," she said. "Did you wish to speak with me?"

Boyd smiled, deepening the creases at the corners of his eyes. "Yes, Miss Daly. Your aid in the apprehension of Mr. Carlyle was rather notable."

Catherine recalled her suspicion of Boyd when he'd first taken management of the print shop. She had thought it possible for him to kill Ainsworth, to have taken the timepiece, when Spencer was at fault all along.

"I did not do so alone, sir. Mr. Nolan was also involved."

"Ah, yes. A reputable young man. It was a shame to hear about his father." Boyd's polished shoes clicked over the floorboards. "There's no need to look so worried, Miss Daly. I shan't dismiss you for something you are blameless in. What you did was commendable."

A rush of relief coursed through her. "Thank you, sir. I was rather hoping you would take that opinion."

His eyebrows rose and his mouth crooked upward. "I'll be in the back office, if you require anything."

The door to the back room clicked shut, and then, galvanized, Catherine went to fetch an apron. She slid out a type drawer on her way back, placing it on the desk and taking up her composing stick.

Bridget grinned, sorting through type in the drawer at her own desk. "You see," she said. "I told you it would work out rightly. It was quite the to-do without you here, Catherine."

"Just as I'd thought. Everything falls to pieces in my absence." She looked at Bridget sideways. "It wasn't as if I disappeared."

Bridget's countenance turned grave. "You could've told me, Catherine—about Spencer. You know that, don't you?"

Catherine fixed her eyes on her composing stick. "And what if I was wrong? I didn't want to worry you."

"Well, if you ever suspect there's a murderer in our midst again, I'd appreciate a note at the very least."

Catherine put a hand to her heart. "I'll do my best."

The following day, Catherine made her way to the watchmaker's shop. She walked with a lightness to her step as omnibuses clattered past on the street. She came to the corner and her eyes alit on the small green-fronted building. What a lovely sight it was, as dear to her now as the print shop. The OPEN sign was upon the door; she stepped inside and looked about at the assortment of clocks, the shine of the lamps against the wallpaper.

Guy Nolan emerged from the back room, pausing at the counter. "Catherine." He grinned. "Did all fare well at the print shop?"

She pulled off her gloves, smiling back at him. "It did. Very well, in fact."

He came around the counter to meet her at the front of the shop. He wore an apron over his clothes, his shirtsleeves rolled to his elbows. "That's grand," he said as he helped her out of her coat. "I'm pleased for you."

Catherine turned, gazing up at him. He looked back, his eyes dark. Carefully, he raised a hand to cup her cheek, his thumb brushing over her cheekbone. "Catherine," he said, and swallowed. "May I kiss you?"

She nodded, wordless. She tilted her face up just as he brought his down. The kiss was soft, earnest, gentle, all the things she knew Guy to be. He pulled back, the color high in his cheeks, and she grinned at him.

Just then, Owen dashed down the staircase. His feet were hard and fast on the steps, in a way that was unlike him. He was no longer a stranger to her, no longer strange. Every day, she knew him better—Owen Smith, the boy she and Guy had pulled out from the grave. A smile lit his face. "Hello, Catherine. I thought I heard you." He darted a look at Guy and said, "I meant to bring it down," before hurrying back upstairs.

"What are you having him do?" Catherine asked Guy.

Guy crossed his arms, tipping his chin up with a smile. "We're going through old watches. I thought it best for him to start with those rather than repairs for clients."

"That's probably wise."

Owen returned with a crate in hand. He brought it into the back room and left it on the worktable. Standing in the doorframe, he looked over at Catherine. "What happened at the print shop," he asked, "when you went back?"

"I still have my job," Catherine told him. "Mr. Boyd thinks what we did is commendable." She met Guy's gaze. "The police have been there. They're likely to pay you a call as well."

And as she was preparing to leave, an officer came knocking at the door. Catherine had already given a statement to the police, but Guy had not, being asleep in their lobby. The officer sat with them in the back room, asking Guy questions and writing it all down. He set down his pen finally and asked, "What of the timepiece? Where is it?"

Guy pulled open one of the desk drawers, lifting out the silver pocket watch. It fit neatly in the palm of his hand, and he showed the officer the cracked crystal. "Do you require it for evidence?"

"No need," the officer replied. "Mr. Carlyle has given us a confession."

Catherine sat back against the sofa, saying little, until the officer took his leave. Guy saw him out, and after closing the door, he turned over the sign. His gaze went from Catherine to Owen. There was a sorrowful cast to his expression; he did not try to hide it from them. These past few days were a weight on all their hearts. He took a deep breath and said, "Let's go for a walk, shall we?"

They went out together into the chill autumn evening. In Fernhill Park, a few leaves still clung to the branches, while others covered the grass in a patchwork of orange and brown. The pond lay still and glistening, the old bridge creaking beneath their feet.

The three of them leaned against it, peering down at the water. Catherine saw their reflections, Guy next to her and Owen on the other side of him. She was reminded of the three of them standing in the abandoned church, the gaping roof above them showing the night sky. She marveled at what they had accomplished since then.

Dusk was settling in, streetlamps glowed in the distance, and through the trees, Catherine could see on to the embankment, as well as the way toward the public cemetery. She'd thought the city so dull and gray, but it wasn't—even as the weather turned bitter and the flowers wilted in window boxes, there was still light and warmth to be found.

EPILOGUE

RAIN SPECKLED the streets as Catherine set off toward the watchmaker's shop. The air this morning was warm with the coming spring, and the city was just waking up. Awnings were lifted, window displays were set out, and mail coaches rattled down the road. When the green-fronted building came into sight, she clutched her trunk tighter, walked a little faster. The OPEN sign wasn't yet upon the door. She knocked, keeping at it until the door opened and Guy Nolan stood before her.

He was dressed simply in a white shirt and a dark waistcoat, a pair of brown wool trousers, a watch chain hanging from his waistcoat pocket. With a grin, he stepped back, gesturing her inside.

"I didn't sleep at all last night," he said in a rush. "This will be an adventure, won't it?"

Guy had been sleeping poorly these past few months. He'd been quiet, working too hard, Owen had told her, barely looking up from his worktable until day's end. Though as the weeks went on, he laughed more, ate better. One evening he and Catherine had taken a walk in Fernhill Park, and he'd told her he'd never been out of the city.

Catherine had received letters from her family all through the winter months. She'd set her mind on taking a stagecoach to visit home, saving up her coins at the print shop for the journey. She'd asked Guy if he'd like to accompany her, and he'd readily agreed.

Now she smiled upon seeing his packed trunk at the foot of the coatrack. "Yes, I believe so," she replied.

Guy put on his coat and gloves and fetched his hat.

Owen appeared in the doorway of the back room, wearing a dark apron over his clothes. He said, "Good morning, Catherine."

"Good morning."

Turning to him, Guy said, "Now, Owen, remember Mr. Everley will be coming by to make sure you're all right. You have the Dalys' address, so you must write if anything's the matter or if anything goes wrong—"

Owen's mouth quirked up. "I'll be perfectly fine. You needn't worry." He looked to Catherine. "You know I'll be all right, don't you, Catherine?"

She nodded. "Certainly you will."

"Well, yes," said Guy, jamming on his hat. "Yes, of course, but—"

"You're going to miss the coach, I think," Owen cut in. His eyes shifted to the clocks on the wall, and they gleamed even in the pale-gray morning light, ticking in unison. "You'd better hurry."

Guy picked up his trunk. He looked about the shop as though seeing it anew, before settling his gaze on Catherine. "Do you have everything you need?"

"Yes." She stepped back toward the door, glancing to Owen. "Take care, Owen."

"Take care," he echoed. "I hope you have a wonderful time."

Guy called, "Goodbye, Owen," and followed Catherine as she stepped outside.

The stagecoach left from a tavern near Elgin Square. It would take them out of the city, stop at a coaching inn for the night, and carry on through the country to the town where Catherine's family lived. They walked quickly through the streets to meet it.

Around the corner, the coach waited at the sidewalk's edge. It was painted yellow, a cheerful contrast to the overcast sky, and drawn by a team of four horses. Passengers were already crowding on, and Guy helped Catherine up into the carriage. Sitting beside each other in the dim, close space, they clasped hands atop the seat.

Guy murmured, "Thank you for inviting me along."

She looked at him. He smiled a soft smile, his dark eyes warm and lovely. She squeezed his hand lightly and said, "Thank you for accompanying me."

"Will your family like me, do you think?"

"Well," said Catherine, grinning, "I'm rather fond of you, so I imagine so."

The carriage door swung shut, the coachman disappearing to take a seat at the driver's box. Guy grinned back. "Are you ready?"

The coach set into motion, horses' hooves clicking over the cobbles.

Still smiling, Catherine said, "Yes."

ACKNOWLEDGMENTS

I'm grateful beyond measure to my agent, Kristy Hunter, and my editor, Karen Wojtyla, for their patience and support as I wrote this book. Thank you for helping me make this story better, and for believing in me.

Many thanks to the wonderful team at McElderry Books for all their hard work, including Nicole Fiorica, Justin Chanda, Greg Stadnyk, Tom Daly, Bridget Madsen, Elizabeth Blake-Linn, and Chantal Gersch. Thank you also to the team at Simon & Schuster Canada, including my Canadian publicist, Mackenzie Croft. And thank you to Miranda Meeks for the gorgeous cover illustration.

A huge thank-you to my family and friends for supporting me and my writing.

To the librarians, booksellers, and readers—I'm so grateful for your enthusiasm and support. Thank you so much.

TURN THE PAGE FOR A SNEAK PEEK AT

Songs from the Deep

THERE ARE THREE SIRENS on the beach today.

I watch them, rosining my bow slowly as I do. The tide comes in, restless and white-capped, pushing at the shoreline. The cliff grass pricks at the thin cotton of my dress as I stand, keeping my eyes trained on the beach below.

They are distant and impassive, marble statues staring out to sea.

Movement is rarely what catches their attention. Sound is how they hunt, what they wait for. Any noise is tenfold more interesting to them than a wave of fingers or shuffle of feet.

I slide my bow across the violin in an open note. The song becomes slower, softer, as I dip into a lower pitch. When I quicken my pace, the violin's sound vibrates through the air, and I feel it humming in my chest, in the soles of my feet. The music is sharp against the noonday stillness, the only sound in my ears.

It is a cool afternoon at that. My breath mists in front of me, my fingers holding stiff to the bow's polished wood. The sirens do not seem to mind the chill. They are folded between a bramble of large rocks, their backs to me—long stretches of pale white skin, dark tangled hair—and one of them leans over, resting her head upon the shoulder of another.

I play by the cliff's edge, allowing music to tumble over rocks and into sea. It's the closest I dare play to the beach, as the melodies may well turn siren ears and eyes in my direction. Nothing wrong with a bit of danger though, when it polishes the notes. I play best on days like this, with the sirens near, before the unending sea.

Perhaps they talk to one another. Yet it's the songs they sing that lure anyone within earshot and without protection. I've seen those rescued taken to the hospital: bloodied from teeth and claws, delirious, all too keen to return to the sea, to the creatures in the depths below. Terrible business for the tourists in the end, and still they come. Every summer. For the scenery or for the sirens, perhaps hoping this year shall be the year when Twillengyle Council finally lifts the ban on siren hunting.

That is the year I dread.

I curl my fingers tighter around the violin to get some life back in them. A few minutes more and I'll pack up. Feels lonely, playing for only three sirens, when I've seen groups of ten or fifteen together on the sand at one time. The wind picks up, biting at my cheeks until I know they're rosy with cold, and the sea's string of whitecaps blacken the rocks with their spray. I skip from one tune to the next in an attempt to find a rhythm.

Each note flies off on the wind—toward sirens who do not even turn an ear in acknowledgment. I touch bow to strings a little more firmly.

When the music falters, I stop. A breeze catches the hem of my dress, flicking it this way and that, while I place my violin into its case. It's a battered little thing, black leather faded and scuffed. My father gave it to me years ago, with my initials stamped along the side.

M. A.

The music of my heart.

Not a very good turn of phrase, as his heart ceased beating only two weeks after. *Or not very good music*, I think, loosening the hair of my bow before setting it inside.

I gather up the violin case and take one last glance down the cliff. The sirens have barely moved. One has twisted around slightly, so I can see the knife edge of her cheekbone. Not enough to see her eyes properly. Before, I have—at the right angle and with enough light—and their wide, dark eyes seem to mirror the deepest parts of the sea.

It was my father who first brought me to them, taught me how to clean salt from violin strings, where to watch sirens without being seen, how to protect myself with cold iron and charms. He showed me an island smeared in blood, and I fell in love with it.

On those days, when the sky was still pink with dawn, my father told me the island's folktales. He brought me to the beach and spoke of the creatures the sea sheltered, of the magic that dwelt on Twillengyle's shores. And when the moon shone overhead, full and bright as a coin, ghost stories were told—the souls of those killed by sirens said to wander the cliffs evermore.

But today is windblown and damp, fog misting around me,

clinging to my dress. These are the days for ballads and sorrow, remembrances of widows standing in my place, waiting on the cliffs, not knowing their husbands had already been swept out to sea. The beach gives way to rocks that rise above the waves like chipped grave markers. It's scenery the tourists adore: dark-green swaths of moss and red-brown grass, the sheer face of the crag stained salt white.

I don't know whether the sirens watch me as I leave, or if the cliff's edge holds a pull of its own. Whichever way, my heart feels leaden as I head for home.

But I have long realized a piece of it will always belong to the sea.

"THE SALT WATER will ruin it."

My mother shuffles around our tiny kitchen, making cakes, and still finds time to pause to lecture me. Often when she begins to repeat herself, I pay her no mind—but the changing weather puts me in an argumentative spirit.

"Evidently not, as it still sings."

She looks at me, disapproving that I've spoken out of turn. The lamplight makes her look more weary than usual. Or rather, my presence has. Her hands are covered in flour, and whatever storm is brewing outside, the smell of baking suffocates it inside. The air is made sickly sweet by the scent of honey and melted butter left to congeal in one of the bowls on the counter. Opening the stove, my mother scrapes another full pan across the grills, before saying,

"Then it would make no difference for you to play at the dance hall."

It would make a world of difference. As she well knows.

"I like playing by the cliff."

"I would much prefer you didn't, Moira. It's dangerous. Not to mention foolish besides." She gives a small shake of her head. "Playing music for sirens—even your father wasn't so senseless."

The cunning retort I was set to offer sticks in my throat. Playing for the sirens fills a dark and hollow yearning, a cavernous desire I've no other way to appease.

My mother's eyes fix on the stove, shining with the knowledge that she has said something insightful. My gaze shifts to the one window in the room. Its lace curtains are drawn back, showing rain clouds heavy on the horizon. The gale will turn the island bleak and wild, the light already failing as darkness settles over us like a nightmare cloak.

My mother says, "We'll need to prepare for the storm tonight."

I don't reply. Her words, like needle and thread, have stitched my lips shut. I stand there, feeling as foolish as she called me, as proud as I know myself to be, until an adequate amount of time has passed to leave with my dignity still intact. I walk down the hall to my bedroom, and in the small space, my mother's words liken to an echo. They scratch themselves into the desk chair, curl against the floral wallpaper, slip between the pages of my books. *Even your father wasn't so senseless.* The walls seem to press close, almost to the point of suffocation, and I need to get out—if only for a little while. I button my coat, take hold of my violin case. Then I'm unlocking my window latch and climbing over the paint-flecked ledge.

As soon as I step away from the overhang, the first drops of rain land in my hair. I start back in the direction of the cliffs, the heels of my boots sinking into the mud as though the island wishes to claim them for itself.

My father used to carry me along this path—when I was little and ankle deep in puddles—on his shoulders where I had a clear view of the horizon, sea and sky coming together to form a blurred line in the distance. My mother was softer then as well. I'd wave a clumsy goodbye toward the house with my handkerchief, while she stood by the door, sending kisses into the air as we set off.

Admiration of the island, of the dangers it held, was always there in my father's stories.

Twillengyle is a place to be embraced with one arm, with a dagger ready in the other hand. To be charmed by its magic is not the same as becoming its fool, Moira. Remember that.

As I turn the final corner, the pathway opens up to the great expanse of the moors. To my left is the lighthouse, a blue-and-white tower clinging to the rocks, and the keeper's cottage attached to it, a modest structure of clapboard siding. The beacon light above circles in a bright arc out to sea, making the sky appear darker overhead. The wind brings with it the clean, cold tang of salt water. My fingers become numb around the handle of my violin case, and it'd be rather pointless to take it out now. I can't even separate the music in my mind from the oncoming gale.

It's not a waste though. I needed the walk more than the music, I think. Fresh air to clear my head. From above, I hear the first rumblings of thunder, and I wonder where the sirens have sheltered, whether they'll take to the storm-ravaged beach come morning. Dawn will be quiet, pale and colorless, after a night streaked with thunder and lightning. September has turned cruel quickly, leaves already beginning to change color and litter the ground.

As I near the cliff's edge, I catch movement in the corner of my eye. Coming up the path from the beach is Jude Osric, his shoulders hunched against the wind, eyes cast down. His red-brown curls poke out beneath his cloth cap, windblown and tangled. I look to the lighthouse before returning my attention to him. Jude is its sole keeper, and at nineteen, he is two years my elder. Before I can decide whether to call out or take off into the shadows, he glances in my direction. "Moira," he says, breathless.

I jam my free hand into the pocket of my coat. Wind howls across the moors, and I narrow my eyes against it. "Shouldn't you be up at the light?"

He makes his way toward me. As he does, I realize Jude looks truly terrified. His eyes are shiny and rimmed with red, his already pale face drained of color.

"You can't be here," he says. "Moira, listen, you need to go *right now.*"

This is quite the opposite thing to tell me if he has any real hope of making me leave. I grab hold of his coat sleeve, and for a moment I see the little boy I used to play with, the one who ran after me on the moors.

"Jude." I swallow hard. "What is it?"

He closes his eyes. Bowing his head, he whispers, so quiet it almost gets lost in the wind: "There's a body." He looks up and gestures back toward the path, hand trembling. "Sirens—the sirens must've . . ."

I try to recall if anyone I know planned to go down to the beach today. I think of the fishermen at the harbor, their families . . .

My fingers dig into the sleeve of Jude's coat. "Who is it?"

"I think it's Connor," he says. "Connor Sheahan."

I look out at the cliff's edge. Dread settles deep inside me, clawing its way from the inside out, pulling me into the black. It can't be Connor—I saw Connor just last week. I was teaching him to play his first reel.

He was twelve years old.

"I'm sorry," Jude continues. "I know—I know you were tutoring him."

I meet his gaze. "Show me."

Jude stares as though I've gone mad. "What?"

"I want to see the body." I grab his collar, yanking him close. "Where is he?"

"I really don't think that's wise, Moira. We need to tell the police. I'll wire them from the watch room and . . ."

Adrenaline shoots through my veins like quicksilver. Before Jude can finish his sentence, I tear away from him.

"Wait—*Moira!*"

Jude makes to stop me, but I'm already racing for the pathway. Below the crag, I pinpoint what I'm looking for fast enough. A smear of red—a color that has no place among the dark waters and wet sand. It's a thin ribbon I track along the beach, a crimson that mixes with the edge of the sea in wavering bands. Then I see a patch of black hair, a white shirt soaked through, pale skin cut and bleeding. The body lies near the path, half buried in blood-drenched sand.

My feet slow as I approach. The smell is almost worse than the sight itself. A harsh, metallic odor burns in my nose, fills my throat until I'm close to gagging.

"Oh God."

It's Connor. Connor as he never should've been—left discarded, a deep slash across his neck. The blood is everywhere, a pool of red, staining the tide.

Nothing makes sense.

Behind me, Jude makes a sound quickly covered by a cough. "Moira," he whispers, and it sounds desperate. "Please, Moira, we oughtn't be here."

The words are a plea, but I can't move. I'm frozen in place, my eyes fixed on the boy I once knew, the boy I'd been teaching. Sickness washes over me, making me light-headed, and I dig my nails into my palm to ground myself against it.

I close my eyes. "This was sirens?"

A gust of wind comes to rip the words from the air. I repeat myself and turn to find Jude standing beside me. "Yes," he says. "I believe so."

I shake my head, whether in denial or anger or some combination of the two. "Can't be."

"We need to tell the police," Jude says again.

"Jude, this—this is *wrong*. What was he even doing here? How did he . . . ?"

I look to the boy at our feet. There are things children are taught on this island so they might survive. Connor knew how to listen, how to be careful, to keep still when it was needed.

He'd been a fine student. Sometimes he'd press on the strings too hard, or his posture got lazy—but he was willing to learn and practiced often. He kept track of his mistakes.

Now I'll have his blood on the soles of my boots.

"Sirens wouldn't have left him here," I mutter. "Why didn't they take him out to sea? Why is his neck cut like that? I don't . . ." A lump forms in my throat, and I stop speaking before the weight of everything crushes me.

Jude pinches the bridge of his nose between forefinger and

thumb. I wonder if the memory of his own family has managed to slip into his thoughts.

"Do you not think it at all strange?"

I force the words out, but it isn't the real question I want answered. What I want is to know why Connor was down here in the first place. My heartbeat is rapid as whatever bravery I had leaches into the sand like the blood at our feet.

Jude's too-pale countenance makes it clear he doesn't have much bravery left either. "A strangeness," he says, "I'm sure the police and the *Twillengyle Gazette* will be most concerned with."

I swallow. "Of course," I reply, yet I can't shake off the sense of *wrongness*. I've seen siren deaths before, read about them in the paper, and this isn't like any of them.

Jude doesn't look back as we travel up the cliff, but I do exactly that. I study the crimson stains in the sand, the small and crumpled form of Connor's body. I've no idea what the police will do with him, but I know this is the last time I'll be able to see him as he was. Only then do I turn away and follow in Jude's footsteps to the lighthouse.

The rain and wind pick up, rendering conversation impossible. My violin case bumps against my leg, a small comfort, as I try not to let my mind wander back to the body we've left behind, to the Sheahan family, who'll soon find out their youngest son was taken from them.

The stone path to the keeper's cottage is cracked through, grass and moss softening the edges. We duck under the narrow overhang, and Jude takes a skeleton key from his coat pocket. The door is bright blue, but chipped in places, paint peeling back from the wood. I wonder when he last painted it. He fiddles with the lock, leaning upon the door before twisting the brass knob. We hurry over the threshold, and Jude swings the door closed, shutting out the force of the gale. My ears ring in the sudden silence.

He leads the way through the cottage, past a heavy oak door, and up the winding staircase to the watch room. Most of its small space is occupied by a desk covered in papers, journals, nautical instruments. A map of Twillengyle hangs from one wall, while another has a window overlooking the nearby harbor. There's no bed, but the room looks lived in, like Jude has taken to sleeping at his desk.

He settles into the chair, shifts a stack of documents to reveal a metal instrument fitted with all sorts of dials and screws. Jude touches a hand to the paddle at one end, clicking it to produce a long series of *dah* sounds. Morse code, I realize belatedly.

In a moment his hand is still. "They'll be on their way," he says, looking out the window instead of at me.

"I suppose we need to wait for them?"

He turns back around, and I see something like relief in his expression. "Yes," he says. "I'd like that—you staying here, that is. If you want."

I smile as best I can. "Thank you."

"I'll make tea, shall I?" The way he says it, I can tell he's grasping for some purchase on routine. I nod all the same, and together we go down into the kitchen.